FIT THE CRIME

The Identity Lie

CORINNE ARROWOOD

Fit the Crime: The Indentity Lie.
Copyright © 2023 Corinne Arrowood All rights reserved.

Text: Copyright © 2023 by Corinne Arrowood, All rights reserved.

This is a work of fiction. Names, characters, places, and incidents, either are the product of the author's imagination or are used fictitiously. Any resemblance to actual persons, living or dead, events, or locales, is entirely coincidental.

Published by Corinne Arrowood
United States of America
www.corinnearrowood.com

ISBN: 979-8-9873642-7-7 (eBook)
ISBN: 979-8-9873642-8-4 (Trade Paperback)
ISBN: 979-8-9873642-9-1 (Hardcover)

Cover and Interior Design by Cyrusfiction Productions.

TABLE OF CONTENTS

A Special Note

The statistics of PTSD are staggering. Many of our Marines and soldiers come home entrenched in the horrors they experienced and the nightmares they cannot escape. If you know one of our heroes that might be suffering from PTSD, contact Wounded Warrior Project, National Center for PTSD, VA Caregiver Support Line at 888-823-7458.

QUESTIONS AND CONSIDERATIONS

*T*he feeling of uncertainty bubbled from his stomach to his soul. Trey's question held gravity in his heart. Was he a good guy who needed to fix the wrongs of the world or a bad guy who reveled in the thrill and adrenalin rush of cold-blooded stalking and killing? And what of this God thing?

Where was God when he hid in the corner of his closet, listening to his father beat the living crap out of his mother? As a boy, he prayed for invisibility with hands clamped around his ears. Where was God once his father turned his menacing violence on him, only ten years old, with nightly ruthless beatings? He'd cried out to this supposed Creator called God. Concerning the horror and atrocities of combat, he knew that was part of what he signed up for, so he gave the God entity a pass on the brutalities of war. There certainly was no sign of goodness there, but that was okay; one wouldn't expect it. His biggest question was, where was God when Trinity was beaten and raped? There were too many twisted fucks out there to claim there was an all-knowing, all-powerful, all-loving God.

His grandparents were the only people who truly cared about him as a child; although his mom tried, she was too weak. His grandmother would tell him, "Babe, God don't like ugly, and He smites evil." At the time, he thought he best not be ugly or evil, but had he become that man?

1

He turned to face the detective. "Trey, I have way too many disputes to believe the story of a loving God. To answer your question, am I a good or bad guy? Maybe ask your God. I've had to do horrible things in my life, but none of it was of my choosing. I suppose I could have looked the other way, but the Marines drilled it into me that it was mine to fix. If there is a God, He's responsible for me being the man I am. He and the Marines." He took a gulp rather than a slight touch to the lips of his tumbler of Glenlivet. "Oh, and to be sure, I've been some motherfucker's nightmare; you can take that one to the bank."

Trey stood and patted Babe on the shoulder. "Ya got some soul searching to do, my friend." Trey looked at Max, the older detective. "You leaving, Padna?"

"Nah, gonna have some of the nightly special. Looks like stewed chicken? Tastes good, I bet." He looked at the big guy, "No worries, Babe, I'm not going to browbeat you like some fuckin' wife. My partner's sometimes too tight-assed. You are who you are, right? I bet you've seen some nasty shit dealing with dem Talibanese. Sick motherfuckers."

"On that note, y'all," Trey smiled. "I'm outta here and heading home to my beautiful wife. Pregnancy gives her a special glow. Max, watch your p's and q's; not everybody wants to hear your opinion." He turned and walked out of Louie's Tap.

Max raised his chin and eyebrows as he curled a finger toward Trinity, then winked with a grin. "Hey, darlin, how 'bout a draft and stewed chicken?"

"Coming your way, Detective."

Babe watched Trinity as she moved to the tap. The sway of her hips and natural sultry ways electrified him, with the spark jumping from his eyes to his heart, igniting a flame below his belt. Since the rape, she'd been a little standoffish and undemonstrative in the bed, all the while claiming she was okay. He felt the difference in her kiss and noticed her usual playful responsiveness turn to stone with his touch. Before, she sizzled with sexual longing, taking every opportunity to climb his body. Trinity was usually

2

the instigator of the over-the-top encounters. His cock was her obsession, not that he ever complained.

Perhaps his girl had the same thing they said he had, PTSD. Maybe she needed help. Just because he wasn't going to be defined by some alphabet diagnosis, maybe her ordeal was a different kettle of fish. If one were to look at the scenarios, the Marines trained him for the issues of combat; no one gets trained for a brutal personal violation. He thought back to when he killed her captor; a quick death was not the ideal outcome. Perhaps slow dismemberment might have felt better, or tying him to a post and watching the alligators slowly consume him. Either way, the fucker would have been terrified and suffered an excruciating demise. A fast death was nothing compared to the pain and agony he put Trinity through.

Max dove into the stewed chicken and rice when placed in front of him. It was as though he hadn't eaten in days. "Shit, they got some good food here. Who woulda thought? I sure wouldn't until I saw you with your nightly dinners, big man." Babe couldn't help but think watching him eat was one of the most unappealing things imaginable, making even the hungriest person lose their appetite. He made an almost grunting sound, a combination of nasal snorts and guttural grunts, defined as disgusting. Max was a nice guy with an astute detective mind; he just wasn't bestowed with the best social graces.

Babe cast his gaze around the perimeter of the bar, a habit he had instilled in him by the Corps. Always be ready. It was one of those nights where thankfully, no one was acting the fool pissing him off. His eyes shifted towards an open door. "Get the fuck out," Babe exclaimed with a smile. His usual pan expression, void of emotion, lit up when a man, maybe five-nine, walked in the door. There was no mistaking the face of his ally, one he'd seen so many times. Babe stood. The man entering looked surprised but smiled with a glint in his eyes as he approached the big guy. They hugged, patting the other's back.

"Chop, what brings you to New Orleans?" Babe turned to the detective. "Max, this is Tim Faraday, Chop to me. He's the best helo pilot to take to the sky and by far the gutsiest." He put his arm around Chop's shoulder with a pat. There was an excitement in Babe that Max had never seen. The most he'd ever witnessed was an upturn of one side of his mouth or a slight chuckle. "This man flew without orders or better judgment to grab our scrambling asses from a terrorist compound or hostile environment on more than one occasion. This one time, after taking out the head honcho, we mowed most of the foot soldiers down, but a few combatants hid with rocket launchers, trying to light up the copter. This guy," he flicked his thumb at the pilot, "he's got stones of steel."

To look at the man, he seemed nothing more than average. Medium to slight stature with hair long enough to be tied up in a knot and sporting a long unkempt beard, the man didn't seem to have an impressive bone in his body.

Babe's military buddy coughed out a laugh, "A lot of hot air. Vicarelli was the shit. You're still one of the strongest motherfuckers I've ever seen. I see you're still working out." Babe tried to include Max in the conversation, but it was evident he was the third wheel and had nothing to add except a few 'no kidding' and 'scary shit' comments.

Babe looked his friend square in the eyes. "So, Chop, what are you doing here? Home's where? San Antonio, if my memory serves me right."

His friend arched an eyebrow. "Still drinking scotch, I see. I'll have one of them." Babe signaled Trinity, ordered his buddy's drink, briefly introduced them, then turned his attention to his pilot friend, who continued to speak. "You remember my wife, Hadley? We moved from San Antone to Pensacola to be closer to her mom. We got a kid now, Jagger."

Still grinning, Babe responded, "Excellent. I remember your wife; in fact, we all thought she was too good-looking for your ass. Where is she? I'm guessing she didn't let you loose to roam the French Quarter on your own." He noticed a sinking look on his friend's face. "Y'all still together, brother?" he waited while Chop gathered his thoughts. Babe told his friend, pointing to Trinity, "That's my lady. I never had one, and well, she's the real deal—smokin' hot, intelligent, funny, and doesn't take shit from anyone; tiny as she is, you wouldn't believe how fast she puts people in their place. I wouldn't cross her. Nope." Babe smiled as he watched her.

Max called Trinity over and paid his bill. "Best damn chicken ever, girl. Better than my Momma's cooking, but don't never tell her dat! Take care of my friend here." He patted Babe on the shoulder. Trinity smiled and nodded. "G'night, darlin'. See ya soon," Max raised his chin with a guy nod to Babe and his pilot friend. "You two behave."

Babe watched as Max left, then turned to Chop, "That man, Max, is a detective with NOPD, and even though he doesn't sound or look like it, he's smart." He inhaled deeply, his chest visibly expanding. "So, you clammed up pretty tight when I asked about Hadley. What gives?"

The guy rubbed his brow with his head held down toward his chest. "I dunno; she's gone. No word, no note, no nothin'. I left for work; she left to drop the kid at daycare. I called her a few times durin' the day like we always do, but no answer. The next thing I know, I get a call from the daycare telling me I needed to pick up my son. I called her work, and they said she hadn't come in or called. It's weird." He looked Babe in the eyes, "Hadley and me been together since high school. We barely argued and even talked about maybe another kid." *Past tense, hmm.* "Something ain't right, Vic. I called the police, but they said they can't do nothing for twenty-four hours at least. The cops said all kinds of things, like maybe she split with another man; it's all bullshit. I'm telling you something's happened to her. I feel it in my bones." His story sounded well-thought-out but contrived and out of whack. *I smell bullshit.*

Hearing Chop talk about his missing wife transported Babe back to the incident when Trinity's ex-brother-in-law attacked, raped, and nearly killed her, forming a lump in his throat and a swell of angered fear in his gut. Just the memory of that day rushed the dread to the forefront of his mind. His stomach twisted as his heart raced. He'd never forget that horrible pain trapped in his chest. He felt for his friend; if his story was true, but why would someone lie like that? "So you came looking for me?

Why? How'd you even know where I was or how to find me? I'm not sure how or if I can help, but I'll do whatever I can, brother. You gotta know something." Babe barely wet his lips as he put the glass to his mouth. His mind was rambling, and mid-sip, he looked over and asked again, "How'd you know where to find me?"

The man sat still, staring into his beer. "Remember Vallas?" Babe nodded with a set jaw. "He told me you came to New Orleans, something about maybe going into the VA. That's where I checked first. When you weren't there, I figured you'd try to get some work, and I know it sounds dumb, but I went to the church over by the square and prayed. I asked God to lead me to you, and then I just walked. I landed here. Haven't a clue, but I did. Man, I don't know what you can do, if anything, but I needed a broad shoulder to lean on. I brought my little dude to Hadley's sister; they live on base. I didn't tell her Hadley was missing." *Too much detail for truth.*

Babe ordered another Glenlivet; Trinity squared her eyes and cocked her head. "Babe Vicarelli, you okay, ma man?" He nodded with a half-hearted smile. Her eyes captured his as though looking through to his soul.

He looked at Chop and asked, "I don't know what I can do, but give me all y'all's information, including her phone number, the sister's number, husband's name, contact info, and address. Include Hadley's work number and work address." He tapped his index finger on the bar top.

Trinity came straight away. "Okay, so I see that tap, tap, tap of your finger; what's up? You got that look, Babe." His eyes shifted to hers with a pensive stare. "Big guy, I can see your mind racing." It was the first time since the day of horror that she felt authentic and not encapsulated in an emotional tomb. He drew a long drink, staring at her over the rim. She flashed a smile that sent an involuntary shiver through his body. One of the patrons banged his mug on the bar; she winked at her man. "That's my cue."

Babe turned toward Chop. His stare was more of a glare; something didn't feel right. He and Chop had been through a lot together, and he couldn't fathom him lying about his missing wife. They'd seen too much to lie to each other. *Why me? What the hell can I do?* "You talking straight with me, Faraday? You know nothing and have no idea what could've gone down or where she might have gone?" He took a mouthful of Glenlivet and sucked in through his teeth; he savored the flavor, all the while thinking. *You didn't answer my question.*

Chop was quick to respond. "Nothing, man. Look, I gotta get back to Pensacola for work; I had hoped you might be willing to help." The man seemed antsy, unable to sit still.

"Yeah, well, write down everything I told you to; I'm hitting the head." What whirled through his mind was that when Trinity went missing, he didn't give a fuck about anything but getting her back. Something felt off, and it bugged him that Chop sought him out. Once again, why?

Returning from the restroom, he asked again, purposefully towering over the man, trying to induce apprehension. "I-I got it all here, everything." Chop's voice stammered.

"One more time, Faraday, why'd you need to find me? No fucking bullshit."

Chop stood and braced himself with a rigid posture. "Uh, um, because you always seem to figure things out. You see the invisible, hear the silent; you got some extra sense the rest of us slobs don't have, that's why. If you want me the fuck out of here, just say the word. I thought I could count on you." The man looked him straight in the eyes.

Babe nodded, "Don't know what I can do, but I'll head to Pensacola tomorrow to grab a vibe. I'll see you, mañana. You got my number now, so call me if she shows back home." They gripped each other's hands, curling their fingers around in a more zealous manner and drawing their bodies closer in a one-sided man bump as Babe put a hand on his friend's back. For all those times Chop saved his ass, he felt an obligatory call to action, still acknowledging to himself the pieces were not fitting.

After the man left, Trinity came over. "What's the deal? That guy looked high, Babe."

The big man cocked his head to the side. "Ya think? High? When I knew him, he wasn't a doper. Some of the guys smoked a little weed and snorted some shit on downtime, but never him. All he ever wanted or talked about was getting home to his wife; now, she's missing. He wants me to help him find her like something bad happened, but he's going back to Pensacola as we speak. I don't get that, but he says he can't miss work." Babe shrugged a shoulder and tipped his head. "He saved my ass numerous times, landing the helicopter in hostile conditions." Their eyes locked. One thing for sure working the bar, she'd seen her share of people loaded on dope. Maybe she was right. "The whole situation is odd and sounds off, but I'm going to Pensacola tomorrow and put my eyes on the situation, talk to people, get my own intel. Who knows, maybe it'll pan with his story. He's doing copter tours over the beach and Gulf."

She wiped down the bar, leaning in, trying to make a point with her directness. "That son-of-a-bitch is worried about his work, and you're gonna call in and head to Pensacola? You damn straight; something's not right. My guess is he's doing more than taking tourists sightseeing. I bet he's running drugs or, even worse, human trafficking, but something illegal. Maybe he screwed with the wrong people and—"

Babe interrupted, "She's collateral until he rights his misdealings?"

She patted the top of the bar, "Don't be surprised to find that's the case."

PENSACOLA

Bound for Pensacola with all the contact info stored in his phone, Babe clipped along I-10, his mind racing in competition with his speedometer. He desperately wanted to believe Chop was on the up and up, but he had a nagging feeling about him showing up at Louie's supposedly by coincidence. He sure as shit didn't believe there was any divine map or angel whispering in his ear leading him to the bar. People were different in the Corps than in civilian life, no doubt. His team was composed of Marines with previous occupations and lifestyles. One had been in law enforcement, another a trust fund baby, and a host of special ops; nobody spoke about their personal lives. The Marines trained them for missions of recon, rescue, and obliteration; they all put their lives on the line equally. Swift. Silent. Deadly.

Not being one to shoot the shit with the team, he'd only heard Tim mention his pregnant wife and then briefly met her once in passing. It's not like they hung out. They weren't even friends; it was a bond like no other, the same as he had with the other Marines he led. They were brothers of war. Hell, every member had their reason for signing up; no one ever asked, and he sure didn't want to get into someone else's mess. They worked well as a team. It was the only commonality, but against the enemy and the difference between life and death, that was all that mattered.

From what he remembered, Hadley was a cute blonde with a foul mouth equal to any of his Marines—she motherfucked with the best of them. Babe got the feeling she may have been trailer trash at one time or maybe even pay-for-pleasure, but he never gave it a second thought. She wasn't his wife, and he really didn't give a shit where she hailed from or what her habits might have been; all he knew was Chop was one helluva pilot and had saved his ass.

Babe's memory flashed back to one of the last missions they'd had together as he drove along the monotonous interstate with its hypnotic th-thump between expansion joints in the stretch of roadway.

Flashback: Operation Condor. The ground quaked beneath his boots as deafening explosions surrounded them, causing unmitigated chaos as they hauled ass to the helicopter. "Go, go, go," Babe remembered himself shouting as they ran from Yashid's complex to the awaiting chopper. A spray of enemy fire whizzed passed them. They booked it. Kellogg fell as a bullet tore into him. Commanding everyone else to continue, he ran back and threw the injured warrior over his shoulder. Vallas grabbed Kellogg as they neared the helicopter, dragging him in while Babe lunged in and signaled the pilot to go. The blood stain bloomed at an enormous pace. They ripped his pants away and applied pressure. "Kellogg, you got this, ma brotha. Chop'll have you back pronto. Hang on, you hear me? Vallas, don't let off the pressure. Gotta get the sombitch home." It was a rough ride back; they had eliminated their target, but he could hardly call it a success, having one of his team wounded. The racket caused by the situation echoed throughout his body.

The memory flooded adrenalin into him. The soar began to deescalate as Babe watched the billboards blip by, reminding him of an upright row of dominoes, one after the other. Each with glamourous images, enticing passing travelers to stop and enjoy paradise while feeding their hard-earned coin into the vast array of blinking lights and nerve-wrenching dings of slot machines. *Yeah, not for me. The house always wins.* I-10 was one of those interstates that had a constant stream of advertisements.

After exiting the Mobile tunnel, he speculated he had another hour. The day was beautiful with picture-perfect blue skies, not a cloud in sight. The drive gave him ample time to stream and ponder thoughts—Trinity's body, which brought on a smile, then Chop and the missing wife. Trinity's comment about the drugs made him consider his comrade's request as something duplicitous. Forty-five minutes later, his GPS alerted his exit was a mile away. He flipped the blinker and exited, turning right toward the beach, followed by a series of lefts and rights—one mile here, two miles there, leading to a tidy subdivision of starter homes. He pulled into the driveway.

The key was under the welcome mat, just as Chop had said. Everything appeared in order; nothing unusual. He picked up a pencil from the kitchen counter, pushing a few papers around with the eraser end in case there was a note or something his compatriot had missed. All seemed clear, so he moved on to the bedrooms. One was clearly a kid's room with a crib and shelves of toys and books, but nothing untoward. The master bedroom appeared standard despite his half-unmade bed. On the nightstand was a picture of Hadley and the boy standing between two identical men, one being Tim and the other having to be his twin, so alike that Babe couldn't tell which man was Chop. *Curious; Chop is a twin, news to me. Hm.*

Next to the tucked side of the bed was a blank pad of paper, but he could detect an impression from a previous note. Taking the pencil, he lightly smudged the indention; it was an address. The penmanship seemed more like a woman's with perfectly rounded letters. *Interesting.* He tore the page and headed out, locking the door and placing the key back under the mat.

Babe set the address in his GPS, backed out of the driveway, and headed out of the subdivision. He followed the directions which led him across town and further inland from the gulf. The last turn was onto a sandy dirt road leading to a dismal trailer park. It wasn't one of those neatly landscaped retirement communities where senior citizens grew colorful flowers and relaxed in gliders on their front porches. Those mobile homes were impeccably clean. No, this was a disgusting shithole with cars on blocks and litter in the yards. Not that Babe could be one to judge with his shoebox apartment, but at least it was clean and organized.

He pulled in front, cutting the loud rumble of his Ford two-fifty. He hopped out and walked to the decrepit makeshift porch.

A feeling clenched inside as he approached the entrance, causing a spasm that took his breath away. The last time he had that sensation of uncertainty was driving up to Trinity's house in Lakeview, not knowing if he'd find her alive or murdered in a pool of blood. Looking at the door, he could have forced it open with a slight nudge, but he didn't. He knocked, no answer. He maneuvered, careful not to step on the cracked boards to avoid going straight through under his weight, then peered in the filthy mud-caked windows. From his angle, he didn't see anyone.

An alarmingly foul smell emitted from the back of the trailer, and he determined he would push through the door, given the ripe odor. As he opened the door, the stench of decay was unmistakable—something or someone was dead inside. Dishes were piled high in the sink, and trash, literal trash, was strewn throughout the living area; it was beyond revolting. Babe put his hand beneath his nose, trying to block the putridity. Scattered across the coffee table was an assortment of drug paraphernalia. An old bent teaspoon, a few lighters, and a crunched bit of wax paper, still partially opened and crusted with minuscule lumps and smudges of dope, lay as they were left. He closed his eyes in disgust. "You gotta be kidding me. What the fuck?" His first impulse was to call Chop and ream his ass if this was the kind of people he and his wife were consorting with, but he continued his plight to find the source of the decaying smell. He entered the open door of the bedroom.

Sprawled across the bed was a dead body, but it wasn't Hadley; the deceased was male. There was no way to tell if a struggle had occurred because the place was in such shambles. He turned his head to an ever-so-slight tickle of noise. With stealth, he approached the closet, slowly sliding the door to the side. A woman sat slumped in the corner, arms draped over her splayed legs and head folded down into her chest. He could tell the woman was alive with the slight twitching of her body. Babe reached inside, grabbed her arm, and pulled her out of the closet. Since he'd only met Hadley briefly, he couldn't swear this was the same woman, but the face resembled what he remembered; this chick was just a bad version of his memory. Her eyes were rolled back in her head with just a slit of the white sclera in view. She could barely move her feet; they dragged like in a stupor or daze, obviously fucked up. Her body went completely limp, like a rag doll; he lifted her and gently put her on the sofa in the living room. She was in and out of consciousness.

He called Chop, "I found Hadley, totally fucked up and barely breathing. I'm calling nine-one-one. I don't know what kind of game y'all are playing. Bro, it looks like she's been here longer than a day. There's a dead guy in this shithole of a trailer with your wife near dead in the closet. Faraday, the man's been dead for some time. I don't mess with drugs or drug addicts; you need to get her some help, and I hope you aren't into drugs especially flying through the air."

Chop hadn't said a word up until that point. "Man, I don't know what you're talkin' about; me and Hadley don't do drugs."

Babe let out a loud beastly noise. "Bullshit. Hadley is barely alive in your dead friend's double-wide." He was beyond pissed, and to think he missed a day of work for this crap.

"Double-wide, what? I got a house about six blocks off the beach." He argued.

"Yeah, I've been to your place. Hadley had this address scribbled on a pad next to what I assumed was her side of the bed. I decided to check it out, and this is what I found. I'm calling nine-one-one and getting the fuck out of here. Not my circus, not my monkeys. Y'all need to get your shit together." He hung up the phone and made the emergency call. He pulled out, went a few blocks down, and just for grins, he programmed

Chop's work address. The system indicated it wasn't valid. He called Chop back. "Motherfucker, where you at right now? Gimme the address." Chop called out his location, but not the one he'd written down for Babe. "I don't know what you're trying to pull, but I'm outta here. Other than your address, is any of the information you gave me even correct? What's your game? I don't have time for bullshit like this. I gave up a day of pay for your shit, and that's what it is."

"W-wait, Go a few blocks down from the Holiday Inn Beach Resort; you'll see the helicopter sign. You can't miss it. Do you have Hadley?" *What? This fucker is delusional.*

Staring out the windshield, trying to decide what to do, he saw police cars and an ambulance fly down the street in the direction of the double-wide. "Fuck, no. I want no part of this." The pilot he remembered was a different man to this piece of excrement. He had no honor, courage, or accountability. He was a liar, a con man, and probably into some sick shit.

"You left my wife there? How do I know where they're taking her?" Babe told him to get a pen and gave him the address of the trailer park. "I can't leave. Can you get her or find out where they are taking her?" The voice coming over the phone sounded practiced and disingenuous. He was trying to put on the act, but it was as pitiful and a waste of Babe's time.

With squinted, angry eyes, Babe stared out of the windshield. "What is wrong with you? No, I won't get her or find out anything. I'm staying as far from that mess as I can. Dude, I took a day off of work to look for your wife as a favor for you saving my ass so many times, but this goes beyond the pale. I found her drugged up in the corner of a grimy closet, and a dead man was less than six feet from her. Wake the fuck up. I've found her; now you need to deal with it. I'm gone. See ya." He threw his phone onto the seat with an intense snarl.

Babe balled his fist and hit the steering wheel. His chest tightened, making it difficult to take in a full breath, and he felt the need to hurt someone; right now, it was Chop. Still staring out the windshield, he saw when the ambulance headed from the direction of the double-wide, so he followed it. Thoughts rolled in his head. *This is insane. It's not mine to do.* He watched as it pulled up to the Emergency entrance. It was a big freakin hospital off the main drag.

Babe pulled off and headed toward the Holiday Inn. Sitting at a stoplight, he looked to the right, and out of the corner of his eye, he saw a man, maybe in his twenties, smack the crap out of a girl sitting in the passenger seat as they waited at the gas pump. They were arguing, she was crying, and he popped her again. Flashbacks to his abusive father streamed across his mind. The guy cold-cocked the girl in the cheek, and her head slumped to the side. He had knocked her out. *Oh, hell no, not on my watch.* The car pulled around the vehicle in front of him and sped out of the gas station. *Game on.* Babe followed as the car wove in and out along the street, then the guy had the audacity to pull into a McDonald's and park. "I got you now, motherfucker." Babe pulled in next to the car. The girl was still out for the count. He rapped on the window, and the guy didn't hesitate to put the window down. The thought rambled through his mind, *so you think you're the shit beating a girl.* Babe could feel the guy's tough-man attitude.

"Yeah?" the man replied in an almost threatening manner.

Babe nodded and grabbed the back of the guy's hair, torquing his head. The snap and grizzle were distinctive. The adrenalin pumped through his body, and it felt good. The driver's head slumped to his chest. "You're welcome, you piece of shit. You are now out of your misery and everyone else's." He walked around the car to his truck and hopped in, continuing toward the Holiday Inn. The Corps had drilled into them that it was their duty to defend those who could not defend themselves, and by all standards, the girl was no match for the driver, so he righted that wrong, and he hadn't the slightest hesitation or guilt. It was his to do.

When he pulled up, Chop was sitting in a lawn chair near the helicopter, stroking his stupid-looking long straggly beard. He had a big red, white, and blue sign advertising his helicopter tour—a hundred fifty per person for half an hour. The copter held three passengers plus the pilot. Four fifty for a half hour, yeah, he was making bank, depending on how many tours he had per day. Right before Babe got out of the truck, a car with a couple pulled up, stopped, and walked toward Chop. Babe waited until he finished with his customers. As soon as the pilot completed the booking, he headed toward Babe's truck.

Babe met him halfway. "She's at the big hospital; it's on the main highway. You can't miss it. Man, I don't get y'all. If it were Trinity, I'd do whatever it took to get her safe and healthy. Fuck, Hadley's the mother of your child." Babe's breathing was intense, like a bull about to charge a matador's red cape.

Chop looked down, moving sand with his feet and hands pushed deep in his pockets. He couldn't look Babe in the eyes. "Hadley is an addict; I didn't want to tell you. Her sister takes care of Jagger because she's always loaded. Look, I love her, but the old her, not this junky whore. She's been bangin' guys for dope. She claims she ain't, but I know what I know. Judge me all you want; there's nothing I can do." He avoided looking into Babe's eyes. He was a liar, a deceiver, and a pretender, not a Marine.

Babe passed his hand over his hair, then grabbed Chop's face raising it so they were looking face to face. "She needs fucking help, and what about you? Truth time. You dealing? Moving drugs in your helicopter? Are you on that shit? Fucking tell me the truth; I'll know if you're lying, and if you lie to me, you'll be a dead man. That, my brotha, is a fact. I won't even think twice about it." Babe's face was a dramatic contrast, pitched red with anger to Chop's pasty white of fear, but he had enough drugs onboard to show an irrational act of bravado.

"Fuck you, Babe." He spun around to walk off when Babe grabbed his arm.

"Now," Babe growled, glaring at him and burning with rage. *Yeah, Trey,* he thought, *I'm a nightmare for a lot of motherfuckers.*

Chop put his hands up in surrender. "Man, I don't know what I want. Yeah, I'm runnin' drugs, but the people I'm runnin' them for aren't the kind you can walk away from and live. They approached me and offered me a deal too good to pass up. Ten grand for a quick jaunt to pick up the product. Hey, ten grand. They gave me an eight-ball beside. Hadley and I partied, but they kept doing it, and before I knew it, she was smoking the shit and going all crazy on me. Big-time paranoia, she got a gun and threatened me. It's been fuckin' scary. Her sister has custody of Jagger, all because of her stupid shit, and now I'm locked in too deep to get out."

Babe looked out at the water, seething with anger but desperately wanting to help a brother from the warzone. He was wracked with disgust but compelled to do something. "Get her some fuckin' help, clean up your act, and move the fuck out of here. I'm pretty sure you don't own the bird. Walk away, sell your house or move out, just get the fuck outta here, go back to San Antonio, but don't darken my doorway with this line of horseshit. Go to the hospital, see her, and give her an ultimatum, get clean, or it's over. If your marriage means enough, she'll get help. Take her straight from the hospital to rehab, and you stop using and moving the shit. Call me when you find your balls. You used to have a set made of steel." Babe turned away and walked to his truck. He turned back, pointing, "You never woulda backed down from anyone. The places you landed for us, shit! Cartel or Mafia, dude? Remember the Taliban? Find your balls."

The whole way home, all he could think about was the sensation he got from ridding the world of the girl-beating punk. The fact was clear. He liked killing and was good at it, but it had never been just for taking a life senselessly. He had no desire to kill for the sake of killing or the thrill; the pieces of crap he snuffed were cruel, abusive, and abhorrent—a blight on the world. That was the source of satisfaction. Dancing between the sheets with Trinity was powerful, but this intoxication was completely different;

instead of a moan of euphoria, it was a feral growl that shook the earth. The warmth from Trinity felt genuine and ignited something in his soul. It was still such a new feeling like none other, and he hadn't gotten used to it yet. *Will I ever be right with it? Am I worthy of her love?*

Instead of a three-hour drive back, it was four and a half with the tunnel traffic and rush hour. As he pulled into an open parking spot on Iberville Street in the Quarter, thoughts ricocheted to gazing into Trinity's eyes. His heart did a quick double beat, and he felt rapturous to be with her. There was life in their relationship, whereas his other passion held death and satisfaction for only one. Nonetheless, it felt invigorating, like he was doing something good for the world, just like in the combat zone. *Demons dressed up like everyday Joes prowl the streets looking for the innocent and are a dime a dozen.* While he knew it was a rambling thought, there was no doubt it was a fact.

When he walked into Louie's, Trinity had her back to him. He watched as she rocked her hips back and forth to the beat of the music. He could use some of that swaying back and forth. Then she stood perfectly still like a deer in the woods that heard a snap of a branch or crunch of fallen leaves beneath a foot. Slowly she turned, and upon seeing the big guy, she sprinted from around the bar. "I called Samantha and asked her to work for me. She should be here in an hour." She curled her fingers in the belt loops of his jeans and yanked him closer so their bodies were touching. "You and me need some alone time to talk and whateva you fancy."

Babe leaned down and lightly kissed her lips. "I'm glad you have blondie coming in. We do need some time undisturbed. No banging mugs on the bar. You and me and nobody else, oh except Gunner. That dog has class. He's totally about being at your place. To hell with my cozy digs." She threw her head back with a hearty laugh.

Trinity bumped her hip into him with a flirtatious giggle. "It's all about the cushy bed, toys, and treats; I assure you—that dog pines for you, ma man, just as hard as I do. I know I haven't shown it recently, but I'm getting real again. I got a lot more head shit to go through, but I'm on my way."

He walked her toward the bar, guiding her with a light touch to the middle of the back, sending chills through him. He took his seat at the end, giving a keen advantage to the comings and goings at Louie's Tap. Her needy customers seemed content and less demanding for fifteen minutes or so. In a few words, he suggested PTSD counseling for her, dancing around that the Marines had trained him for the stress of combat. There was no such training to equip someone for a personal accost like she'd experienced. Rape, kidnapping, and physical assault weren't the standard by social protocols in life. Their eyes connected with intensity. Babe wasn't sure if she was positioning for a full-blown stand-off or if she was considering the suggestion. Her lips turned up with a coy smile.

"Can I get a short drink, Trinity? You're not gonna believe the shitstorm in Pensacola; well, maybe you will because you pegged the drug situation balls-on-accurate." She smirked with an I-told-you-so attitude and sashayed to the back bar for Glenlivet. Trinity gazed at him as she walked the drink back.

"Not gonna say told you so, but—" she smirked.

"You told me, and you were right. The mess in Pensacola is crazy. In combat scenarios or hanging around base camp, we see different sides of each other, but once out of the land of destruction, there's the real-life side. Some of us come back more fucked up than others, but I don't think anyone comes back whole. In the Corps, it's a different world, Trinity, laser-focused and yet surreal. It's hard to explain-it's a total head space thing, plus I'm not what you would call a social animal."

They both turned when Samantha entered. Her voice was loud and laced with drama. Everything was a lemme-tell-ya. "Told ya I wouldn't be long now y'all go do whateva it is you do." She winked at Trinity, "I got this for you, girl. Enjoy your man." Trinity shoved her tip cash in Samantha's pocket and grabbed her things.

"Thanks, girl. I owe you." Babe drained his glass, joined Trinity, and they headed out.

As they walked into Hotel Noelle, Lex, the evening reception manager, greeted them. "Neville wants to talk to you." He handed the phone to Trinity.

"Did Dad get you?" he asked.

Her expression darkened with fear. "No, is everything okay?"

"Yeah, all's well; he wants to talk to Babe."

"Odd. We'll call him in a little bit. Why, I wonder?" *What a weird request*, she thought.

The phone rang, and she handed the phone back to Lex, who punched another button. "Hotel Noelle, how may I assist you? Hold on; I'll connect you." He pressed a few buttons and looked back up at them. "Hope everything is okay." Trinity nodded, smiled, and waved as she and Babe walked away.

They proceeded through the hotel to her apartment. Babe could hear Gunner prancing with excitement at the door. "Good boy," Babe said as Trinity swiped the card to unlock the door. He patted Gunner's back and grabbed his leash along with a few treats and a poop bag. "You coming for the walk or putting your feet up?" Babe asked Trinity. "We're gonna walk to Armstrong Park, maybe pass by the job site for a minute or two. Coming or staying, either way, our boy needs a walk."

Trinity started stripping off her clothes as she walked toward the washing machine to drop them inside. "Y'all go. I'm jumping in the shower." Babe eagerly watched as she removed her clothes. "Don't even think about anything until I get this bar grunge off; I'm disgusting. Y'all go for your walk, and then I'll shower again with you. I'll make it worth your while." She did a slow bat of her eyes before turning into her bedroom. She sizzled with heat, making him think twice about the walk, but Gunner wasn't relenting, and a walk was of the highest calling.

Babe hollered, "It'll be a quick walk, maybe just around the block." He looked down at Gunner. "Let's get your business done and fast. No sniffin' every square inch of the block." They headed out the back door.

After a successful fifteen-minute walk, they returned to the apartment. Trinity lounged on the sofa in an oversized Saints tee shirt with the TV rolling one of the news channels. "Would you look at this shit; the city tore down another statue." Her face contorted in disgust, with one side of her lip tweaked upward. "It sickens me what they're doing to my city. Reparations, what? I bet those idiots with the signs don't even have a lineage to any slaves. Ya know, it's way way back, but my Mama's side has slave heritage. I can promise these peeps don't have a clue what it means to work their asses off. Ignorant. Ignorant. Ignorant." Then she mumbled under her breath.

Babe filled Gunner's bowl with water and then made his way to the bedroom. "You gonna shower with me, or was that a tease?" he called over his shoulder as he began stripping his shirt off. Unlike the whirlwind of a mess in her bedroom with clothes strewn everywhere, he folded his shirt and jeans on the bathroom counter, turned on the shower, and stepped in. The water beat on his back. He closed his eyes, trying to relax, but flashes of the morning came to mind. It was hard to fathom the bullshit some people had in their life. Then a visual montage of the guy smacking the girl in the car stormed to the front of his mind. The more he thought about ending the guy, the more his body excitedly reacted.

In a soft, sultry voice, Trinity commented, "Oh. I see you're already thinking of me." She pressed her body against him. He lifted her against the shower wall. "Slow down, big guy. I want you desperately but not in a wham-bam-thank-you-ma'am way." He didn't stop, and as the pulsing began, he loudly moaned.

He breathed along the side of her neck. "I promise, Trinity, this won't be one and done. My body has been aching for your passion." How could he tell her the excitement came from remembering a cold, calculated murder? Just the thought started, his blood coursing through his body. *Stop, dammit,* he thought. "Let's go to bed."

They lay in the bed, heads propped on pillows facing each other. Babe studied her face. She was beautiful with tiny features. Most of the bruising from the day of torture had faded. "So, Vicarelli, tell me about your morning and how I was so right." She fluttered her eyelashes with a sarcastic grin.

"I think I have better things to talk to you about." He raised one eyebrow. Babe rolled on his back, pulling her on top of him. "How about I start by telling you how sexy you look? I love your tits and bits." He caressed her breasts, gently tightening his grip. "Oh, yes, Miss Trinity. For being so tiny, you have a great rack. Perfect. She leaned toward his face, honing in on his lips, delicately kissing him. Babe drew her closer for a more passionate kiss. "When I first walked into Louie's, the first thing I saw was you rocking your hips back and forth. I immediately thought I'd like to get some rocking on me, and here you are. Girl, you gonna rock my world?"

NOT FOR SALE OR HIRE

*A*fter an hour of playing around, Trinity reminded Babe. "Why does my dad want to talk to you? Don't think you're getting off the hook about today's adventure to Pensacola and, oh yeah, how I was so right about your compadre. I guess you gotta call Dad first, but then I want the whole story."

He chuckled, saying, "The whole story?" His eyes darted back and forth as he gazed into hers. "I'm not so sure you do, but we need to call; however, I cannot and will not talk to your dad while I'm naked in bed with you." She laughed.

Donning her Saints tee shirt and sleeping shorts, she watched as he put his clothes on, tucked in his shirt, and buckled his belt. "Are you going to put your shoes on too?" She nudged him in the ribs. "Sometimes you are regimented to the core, but then other times," she put her hand on her hip and made a sizzling noise, "You are nasty in the best of ways, and to think I'm your first girlfriend. I'm one lucky lady."

He tossed her his phone. "I don't have your father's number. Will you please add it to my contacts?" She grinned.

"Yes, I will add my dad to your contact list, but I expected some rebuttal like," and she lowered her voice to a deep male tone, "Yes, Trinity, maybe you're my first girlfriend, but I've had women all around the world." She followed him out of the bedroom. He turned and smiled with a gravelly chuckle.

He grabbed a bottle of water from the fridge and sat on the sofa, patting the spot next to him. He hit the green dot, and her dad's phone rang. It was his private line.

Her dad answered, "Antoine Noelle."

"Mr. Noelle, this is Babe Vicarelli. Neville told me you wanted to speak with me. How can I be of assistance, sir?" His eyes jetted toward Trinity, who was suggestively tickling him, rubbing her hands all over his body.

"I thought you and I could meet in person. Do you have time tomorrow or the next day?" While pleasant, the man was all business.

Babe raised his eyebrows at Trinity in disbelief at her actions. "Yes, sir. I work from early morning and knock off at seventeen hundred, um five. I might be able to break away around twelve, sir, at lunch."

"Let's make it five thirty tomorrow at my office." While sounding easy enough, there was an underlying edge to Mr. Antoine Noelle's voice.

"Yes, sir. Is that on the third floor?" Babe asked while frowning at Trinity.

"I'll have someone bring you up."

"Tomorrow, then, sir."

The call ended. "That is weird. Why does my dad want to talk with you?" She looked down, twisting stray threads from the hem of her shorts. "Babe, please don't think, uh, never mind."

"Girl, I felt disrespectful talking to your father as you took advantage of me. Want a water?" He stood, stretched, and made his way to the kitchen. "You started a party in my pants. That was underhanded and could've made for an embarrassing situation." He waited for some smart-ass comeback.

"No, a glass of wine, please." He poured the wine and sat back on the couch. She had her legs tucked under her, took the offered glass, followed by a few small sips, and turned on the television.

The clock in the hall ticked away the seconds as he rehearsed the words he wanted to say. Should he say something or let it be? She propped her feet on his legs, encouraging a touch. He held her foot, applying pressure to the curve of her arch with his thumbs. She could tell he was contemplating something, but his thought process was anyone's guess. He started to speak a couple of times, then cleared his throat.

"Trinity, I've heard talk, and I know some of your dad's business ventures may not be above board, but ya know, it's not mine to judge. I sure as shit wouldn't throw any stones. Your dad knows the kind of man I am without even speaking. In some ways, we are alike. We take care of our own, and with you, he and I have a common interest." He lightly kissed her on the nose.

"Would you stand up?" He stood as she undid his belt, unfastened his pants, untucked his shirt, and said, "Now, you look a bit more relaxed." She giggled like a schoolgirl.

They cozied on the sofa, watching an episode of The Sinner on Netflix. She climbed on his lap, taking his face between her hands as though studying it. "Babe, anyone ever tell you, you could be a model or a movie star? I mean, you got high cheekbones, beautiful eyes, killer lips, and a great smile, even though it's a little crooked, but I think that's sexy. Oh, not forgetting your jaw and that totally chiseled look, even though it's hidden beneath this." She grabbed a handful of his trimmed beard. "Most huge guys look jar-headish, but not you." She squinted while gazing into his eyes and pecked him on the lips. "You never did tell me about your buddy."

"Shh. Watch the show."

Work came too early, but he got up and went through his morning workout routine, then he and Gunner jogged to the construction site. The project was moving along, and Glenn, Babe's boss, hadn't said anything about him taking off a day or leaving at odd times, but he knew he'd get taken to task eventually. It was bound to happen; if it were one of his people, there certainly would be consequences.

Gunner bounced up to the trailer for Glenn's treats. "Hey, boy." Glenn ruffled his fur while Gunner smothered him with affection. The dog had become part of the crew, and they spoiled him with rawhide, treats, and balls. "I missed you yesterday, pooch. Got you a new bag of chews." The site super handed the dog a treat. Babe clocked into work. "Everything okay with you, Vicarelli?"

"Yes, sir." He looked over at Glenn. "Sorry, I had to help a guy I served with yesterday. It won't happen very often."

"Vic, I told you, and I meant it, you'll have a job with me as long as you want it. You let me know, that's the important thing. Hell, you gotta help one of your guys out; not a problem. Your Marine need a job?" He was playing tug-of-war with the dog.

"No, sir. Not muddying the water just yet." He leaned against a table across from his boss' desk. He ran a hand down his face, taking in a deep breath. "The guy's got problems; until he sorts them out, I don't have any more time for him. People looking for trouble will generally find it. I helped him yesterday, but until he gets his shit together, I won't go down that hole. Not trying to be heartless, but we all make our way, and we all got baggage. I just don't need to carry his until he tries to haul it himself; then I'll help."

Glenn understood and could appreciate the sentiment. Babe put his hard hat on and went to work while Gunner snoozed in the office trailer. Throughout the day, he couldn't help but wonder what Trinity's dad could possibly want with him. Their only conversation until that point conveyed gratitude for saving her from her ex's deranged brother and a quick inquiry questioning if anything needed cleaning up. Without going into detail, both men understood the nature of the conversation and the unspoken words. He hoped Mr. Noelle wasn't looking for someone to take care of problems that got in the way of his business. Being someone's muscle wasn't his jam. Taking trash from the streets or eliminating a threat was a whole different thing; there wasn't anything self-serving about his propensity to right wrongs. Yet, it did give him a sordid sense of pleasure.

The food truck, a new alternative for lunch, pulled up to the site. The men quickly formed a queue rattling off their orders. Burger and fries seemed to be the staple of the day. Sitting in the shade, Glenn joined him. "No burger and fries for you? Fish tacos from a food truck? I hope you don't get ptomaine poisoning." Glenn took another bite of his hamburger. "I heard the guys talking; stop me if I cross a line. You dating Trinity Noelle?"

Babe looked off into space while he chewed the tolerable fish taco. "Yes, sir. Nice girl."

"You know who her pop is? I'm surprised he hasn't vetoed the relationship. No offense, but I think he's hoping for a legit businessman or man of means, not a soldier turned construction worker. In the Quarter, the Noelle family is like royalty." He munched a fry with rabbity-like nibbles.

"Yes, sir, I'm aware. Who knows? Safe so far." Babe pushed the last bite of the fish taco into his mouth; all that remained were tortilla strips. He started thinking the fish may have been a poor choice. He sure didn't want to deal with visits to the Pot of Gold. "Trinity and I have a good thing. I never got a feeling that he disapproved; time will tell, I suppose." He stretched his neck with his head leaning toward his shoulder, slowly going back and forth a few times. "She's good to my dog."

"Oh, well then, it's gotta be love in paradise. Hey, I feel like Gunner is a step-child to me." Babe laughed at the comment.

"Aww, you hear that boy?" He handed Gunner the tortilla strips from his taco and tossed the paper in the trash.

While sometimes amusing, the constant chatter of the men at the site could also get wearisome. He didn't need to hear about who was getting laid, blown, high, drunk, or cavorting. It was always someone trying to one-up someone else, and it grated on his nerves, but he held his silence.

It served to make the day, particularly then, move faster, and five o'clock rolled around not a moment too soon.

Babe brought Gunner to Louie's. Trinity whispered, "Good luck with my dad. I'll want to hear all about it, so don't forget a word, okay?"

Babe whispered back, "I won't." Perhaps, his stomach should be in knots, but he'd never met a man he was afraid of, and today wasn't going to be the day to change that. His stomach rumbles had more to do with the fish tacos melded, perhaps, with curiosity.

Bang on five-twenty, Babe crossed the threshold of the Hotel Noelle. He didn't have time to sit before Neville, Trinity's oldest brother, approached. "Hey," they shook hands, "Follow me." The office was indeed on the third floor, but it was down passageways and seemed to be two stories over Trinity's apartment. His mind wandered, wondering how many or if any of her siblings lived at the hotel and how many times her dad had been sitting at his desk while they were getting busy on the first floor. *Hmm.*

Sitting at an antique chestnut desk, easily from the eighteen hundreds, sat a pretty blonde-haired lady, perhaps in her late forties. She had a pleasant smile enhanced by bright pink lipstick, which accentuated the whiteness of her teeth. "Rose Marie, this is Mr. Vicarelli, a friend of the family." Babe nodded with a smile as she said hello. He was always aware of his surroundings and careful to notice people's body language. So far, her family had been nothing but gracious and authentic. The night of Trinity's terror, her dad was forthcoming and direct. There wasn't any ambiguity in their question-and-answer moment. "Rose Marie runs the show; my dad just thinks he does." They all politely chuckled at the gesture. Neville pointed to a heavy-looking closed door. He lightly knocked on the door and opened it, ushering Babe in with a flick of his wrist.

Her dad stood when Babe walked into the office. "Please come take a seat. Would you like a cold drink? Coffee, water? Or something stronger?" Mr. Noelle had a welcoming but all-business smile on his face as he spoke to Babe. Antoine Noelle had a head full of black wavy hair with shimmering silver streaks running amidst the darkness. Unlike Trinity, he had pale eyes, like some of her siblings, and a thin but wide smile, not the full puckers of his girl. There was an unspoken intensity about the man.

"No, sir. You have questions for me?" The two looked eye to eye. *No beating around the bush, please,* Babe thought.

"No. I wanted to get to know you better since you spend so much time at my daughter's place. I like to know something about the people under my roof, so to speak," arms bent at the elbows and palms up, he shrugged his shoulders with a gentle nod of his head. "My daughter is a grown woman, and I know you are aware that she was married, but she's still our baby girl. Did you know she is the baby of seven? God has blessed us with many children and grandchildren."

"Yes, sir, I've met some of the family." He politely smiled.

"Tell me about yourself." He had a pleasant tone in his voice but an expressionless look about him. Babe had an inward sigh, thinking to himself, *we both know what this is about, but I'll play the game for Trinity.*

Babe clasped his hands in his lap. "I'm basically a local guy; grew up in Mid-City and uptown. My father is a son-of-a-bitch; he abused my mother and me until I was twelve, and I ended that. Wrestled on scholarship in college, graduated from law school, and joined the military—"

Her father interrupted, "What branch?" He asked, almost amused.

"Marines, sir."

"You ever deployed?"

"Yes, sir. Many tours, and I was part of the Special Operations Command. I'm a Raider. I was in the middle of combat and other activities that I am not at liberty to discuss, sir. Besides, it doesn't make for good conversation." There were some things he could talk about, but that wasn't the point of this exercise.

"So you had no problem taking care of the issue we had not too long ago?"

With a raised eyebrow and a slight smirk, Babe responded, "Not in the slightest, sir."

"Uh-huh." Mr. Noelle briefly nodded.

"If I may speak candidly, sir, I have no problem in that area and am more than capable when injustice occurs, such as the situation to wit we refer. The Marines trained me to fight for those too weak to fight, punish those that needed punishment, and protect our country and way of life. My team and I put it all on the line, even if it meant our lives. I can assure you that nothing I do or have done has been for self-indulgence."

A smile slowly crept across the man's face as he listened to Babe. The Marine had made his point without having to say, 'I won't be a hitman or strongarm for hire.' "I can see that you and my daughter are getting close. Is it your desire to marry her?" Babe cocked his head, thinking, *where is this going?*

Once again, there was an uncomfortable, elongated pause. Babe casually responded, "I don't know how to answer that, sir. Trinity and I have never spoken on the matter, and I think she would tell you it's premature. I will say to you she is the first lady I've ever loved. That's huge for me." He looked her dad directly in the eye, punctuating the comment by placing his hand over his heart.

"What, you just had friends with benefits? Or what? Hookers?" Now it was Mr. Noelle's turn to cock his head turning the tables. *What the fuck does he care?*

Babe felt a knot of resentment developing in his stomach. This guy was asking too many questions just to get to know him. "Finding someone to have sex with has never been an issue, and I'm not sure I understand the need for this conversation, not to be rude. Trinity knows she's my first girlfriend. I've never been a people person, as they say."

"I meant no disrespect. I asked like man to man, and please call me Antoine." Babe thought, *No can do, not yet anyway*. "I own the construction company you work for; it's one of my many businesses. Construction in the Quarter, the Marigny, and Treme can be tricky with all the red tape. The zoning commissioner and inspectors never give me problems like they do other construction companies working in the area. We're friends. I can be helpful to those wanting to climb the ladder." Antoine leaned back in his chair. *Point made*.

Babe relaxed in his chair, as well. Plain and simple, the guy wanted to buy him and his unique skills; the problem being he was not for sale. "You've given me much to think about, sir. I don't, as of now, know the construction business enough to move up, but I am a quick learner, and if I find that I might want to further my position, it is good to know I can always talk to you."

Mr. Noelle stood, indicating the meeting was over. "I gotta ask you, is your actual name Babe or is that a nickname?" Babe stood and let out a staggered chuckle.

"Yes, sir. Babe is my real name. My grandfather named me after Babe Ruth."

The man clasped his elbow, "You do know his name was George?"

"Yes, sir."

"I suspect we will be family one day, and I need to know if you will be loyal to this family, Babe?"

The big guy turned to face Trinity's father looking down at his medium stature of five-nine. "Sir, I am loyal to a fault." *But I'm not going to kill or maim for you, motherfucker*, he thought.

"Good to know." He patted Babe on the arm and opened the door. "We will speak soon." His eyebrows knitted together for a look of sincerity and an attempt at warmth. "Have Trinity bring you by the house for Sunday dinner. You go to Mass on Sunday? You two will have to join us. We go as a family, and there's a lot of us." Babe smiled and shook his hand before leaving.

The questions posed by Antoine rolled through his mind. He dissected every answer as he walked to Louie's. What could he tell Trinity? Your dad's a thug in a five-thousand-dollar suit. He wondered if she had any idea that he wasn't just an entrepreneur that owned a hotel and a couple of businesses. No, the dude had commissioners, inspectors, and probably every city official in his pocket. Certainly, Shep knew, and what about Trey and Max? While Trinty had gathered street smarts and could spot the questionable ways of others, perhaps she was blind to her father, and Babe wasn't going to be the one to crush her dreams. Nope.

When he rounded through the open door at Louie's, Gunner ran up to him, wagging his tail fiercely and glued to his side. "Everything okay here?" He stroked Gunner's fur. "You watching them?" Babe tilted his head to the right, and a cluster of men, eyeing Trinity waiting for their beverages. She had a tray filled with drinks ready to carry to the table.

Finn, one of the bussers, ran to the bar. "I got this, girl. I seen how those pricks were sizing you up, and now, with the Hulk here, it's not gonna be a pretty sight if they get too mouthy or handsy."

The men were seated around three tables shoved together. They had the appearance of mid-westerners shocked by the depravity of the French Quarter yet enjoying the eyeful of it all. He'd served with many mid-westerners, who always seemed innocent when they first deployed, probably even more so before boot. Nonetheless, these guys were grown-ass men, and Trinity was smokin' hot; he'd keep a close watch on the behavior. As Finn approached, Babe read the disappointment on their faces that it hadn't been the sexy bartender. *Just as well,* he thought.

He turned his attention to Trinity and watched as she sashayed from

32

behind the bar oozing with sex appeal. "Hey, handsome," she called out to Babe with a seductive gleam. She stretched on her tip-toes with her arms balanced on his shoulders. "Come here, you." She looked at his lips, then his eyes, and back again to his lips, tempting him into a quick kiss. Just for shits and giggles or maybe to mark his territory, he put his hand on her ass. "Making me a promise for later, Vic, or just being a tease?"

He leaned down and kissed her again. "Just playing," he looked over her head at the table of men. Yep, they'd seen the kiss, the ass-grab, the size of the beast claiming his territory, and they all knew she was off-limits.

Babe took his usual seat at the end of the bar and ordered a Caesar salad. Given the tacos from earlier in the day, he thought he should go simple but made sure to have his two-finger pour of Glenlivet. Finn brought him the salad. "All you getting is this salad, Babe? Surely you need more calories, a big guy like you. How about I bring some grilled chicken or shrimp to go on the salad?"

"I'm good, Finn. How's it going? After all the crap during the spring with those college kids, I was surprised you stayed here. That was some kinda shit. No offense, but I don't get your generation." He seasoned his salad.

The busser laughed, "I don't get my generation. We got a bunch of freaks; you don't know the half of it." The tray tucked under his arm, he continued, "Those Ole Miss kids were up to some kinky shit. I still can't believe that girl Jessica died; from what I heard, it was some sort of group sex. She was a sweet girl, and it blew me away that she invited me to her hotel room. Sorry, she died, but happy I wasn't there when it went down. I don't get into all that group stuff. F-heck, no. Better get back to work. One day I'd like to talk to you about the military. I been thinking about enlisting, getting my degree on the army's dime."

As Finn started to walk away, Babe said, "Go Navy, three hots and a cot, if you decide to enlist, but as screwed up as the world is now, I suggest just keep on doing what you're doing." Finn acknowledged with a nod but continued to the other side of Louie's.

ILLUSIONS

The night dragged on; he knew Trinity was anxious about his conversation with her father and was curious to hear the details. Even Gunner seemed antsy. Babe flagged Trinity, "Gunner and I are gonna stroll the streets."

"Troll the streets?" She tilted her head to the side with an inquisitive and annoyed expression.

"No," he repeated, "Stroll, like walk. Troll, what the—" he grinned. "Girl, you know me better than that. There's only one I want." He winked at her. "Come on, Gunn."

They headed out the door. Most passers-by smiled at the dog, a few wanted to pet him, and some made a point to cross the street to escape the animal. They turned onto Royal Street, and he slowed as he approached an antique jewelry store sparkling and glistening with a display of diamonds and precious jewels. The exquisite collection reminded him of his grandfather's brown leather box with his mom's and grandmother's engagement rings and diamond wedding bands. Her father's words rang through him. *Marry?* Hell, they were just figuring out what made each other tick.

There was a loud pop directly behind them, making Gunner start growling and snarling. Babe's reflex kicked in, and he began to move but took a deep breath and turned, expecting nothing more than a vehicle that had backfired. Instead, he saw a person tumble flat out, half on the sidewalk, half in the street, and only several feet from him. Things seemed too quiet and sparse for that time of the evening; it was only nine or nine-thirty. Royal Street was usually teeming with pedestrians. No one was running away, and there wasn't a car speeding off. The perpetrator had either vanished or was part of the three people calmly walking by the downed man with zero recognition of the victim. Babe turned his attention to the injured young man bleeding from a bullet in the gut. He applied pressure and called nine-one-one. Once again thrown into the middle of a crime scene when all he wanted to do was walk Gunner and get back to Trinity.

While Babe forcefully held the guy's bunched-up shirt tail to restrict blood flow, it occurred to him that he was getting control of his over-the-top imagined threats, highly tuned perceptions, and unreasonable reactions. He was thankful that the terrifying nightmares and hallucinations had slowed, not disappeared entirely, but were no longer an everyday occurrence. Memories washed to the front of his mind like waves crashing upon a seawall. He remembered hearing a similar pop on his way home months earlier. Upon hearing what he perceived as gunfire, he thrust himself into combat mode, diving between two parked cars, scrambling for cover with his pulse bounding and senses ready to go on the offense. His senses heightened and keened on reaction; he realized the threat was none other than a car backfiring. Now, had he lost his edge, or did he feel more stable? Was it Trinity's influence, or was he getting a grip that he was out of the fray? *PTSD, what?*

The officers pulled up, as did Trey. "Heya Babe, ya know, maybe you should go into law enforcement." The detective added. "You have a knack for being in the wrong place at the right time or the right place at the wrong time. The EMTs are seconds away."

Looking up from his crouched position, still compressing the wound, Babe replied. "What can I say, Trey? I'm just walking my dog, minding my business. I heard this pop; for the first time in a long while, I didn't duck for cover or clamber around a wall. Wouldn't you know the one time I sluff it off as a backfire, it's a fuckin' gunshot. If I had been paying attention, I would have known it was a gun, but I was more interested in a conversation I had earlier and in Gunner getting his business done. I didn't get a hint or an indication of the shooter. Three people walked by and acted like they didn't see the guy. The young man is injured but not dead; maybe he can give you some insight." The paramedics pulled up and took over. Although unbelievable, the blood was only on his hands and washed up to his wrists. A few specks splattered his jeans, but nothing compared to many other times when he'd held life-saving pressure or tied a tourniquet.

"Like I told you," Babe stood with the leash in one hand and the other on his hip, "There wasn't a car anywhere around, which is strange, and the only people were the group of three. I was paying attention to the kid who was down, but I think I saw them take a right a couple of blocks down— one female blonde with a purple jacket and shoes." He tipped his head and focused upward like trying to recall the images. "The guys were average, like five-ten, one-seventy, I'd say. Brown hair, one in jeans, the other in khakis, both in tailored shirts, blue, I think. That's all I can tell ya; look, I gotta bail. I did my part."

"Go, I got your number." By this time, the paramedics had an open IV running, rolling the victim into the wagon. "Hey, any chance the shooter missed and was gunnin' for you?"

"Trey," one side of Babe's mouth turned upward. "I'd get my money back if I hired an assassin to take me out, and they hit the guy behind me—they sure as shit wouldn't be a very good gun for hire to miss me. I'm a sizeable target, and all my attention was on Gunner and hoping he'd lift a leg, not scanning for shooters." Babe scoffed.

Talking to the dog, he looked down, "Come on, you need to do your thing, boy." They walked to the corner, turned, and continued around the block. The rest of the walk, Babe played the loop of the gunshot and the guy down. He tried to force his mind around the scene like a periscope doing a 360. He berated himself for not seeing the shooter; maybe he was settling into civilian life too much. With his propensity wanting to right wrongs, it was a luxury he couldn't afford. There were too many sickos on the streets; he had to protect those going through life unawares. Maybe there was something he'd missed walking Gunner that could have saved the guy from being shot, and perhaps if he hadn't been thrown off by Antoine eluding to marriage, he'd have been more on his toes.

The thing about being a big man was that he was an easy target, and for some reason, so many people wanted to buck up to him, like proving a point. In the Corps, there were much smaller men in ops that could've kicked his ass, no doubt about it. Yes, was he a force to deal with, undoubtedly. Was he highly skilled and, at times, beyond motivated? Hell yes. He coughed out a laugh at Trey's comment and declared, "You bet I'm some motherfucker's worst nightmare."

"Give me the fuckin' gun; your hands are shakin' too much. How the fuck did you miss the guy? He's a giant ass target. Who paid you to do the hit? Look, I'll do it, and you give me half." The shooter slid down the wall to the floor with a blank gaze, the SR-25 sniper rifle slipping onto his lap. The man talking kicked his foot. "Get a fuckin grip; it's a job, nothing personal. If you can't do it, tell you're money man you know someone who can." Hatred and hostility pierced the night as the assassin looked with disgust at his accomplice. The man raised his hands, "Not sayin' nothin'; I see the shakes in your hands; maybe you need a quick fix. I ain't doggin' you, no. I ain't never been paid to take someone out, just sayin'. Tryin' to help, bro."

With a guttural grumble, the man climbed to his feet and said, "Next time." The two men left through the back alley next to a two-story building and slinked into the night.

Trinity stood at the door, looking out from side to side with her hands on her hips. Her face lit up as Babe and Gunner made the corner. She watched as they quickly moved toward Louie's. "Starting to worry about you two."

Babe smiled at her. "Gunner's a good boy. He did the whole shebang. Here we are, walking along, trying to get around the block for his due diligence, when pop, I think I hear a backfire. Nope, just behind me, a little more than arm's length, this young guy is down, shot in the gut, laid out half in the street, half on the sidewalk. Thinking back on it, he must have been crossing the street. I helped until the paramedics got there. Oh, and Trey pulls up and has some smart-ass comments." She looked at his hands, seeing the glove-like blood stains. "Yeah, I gotta wash up. Gunner was a champ, though, stood by my side while I tended to the kid. It's always something; all fun and games around here." Trinity unleashed Gunner, and the pup curled at the base of Babe's stool, waiting for his master to return from the bathroom.

An hour later, sipping on his second two-finger pour, he could feel the tension leaving his neck and thoughts of sleep entering his mind. Trinity looked over at her man; his eyes had that I'm-ready-for-bed look. She sauntered over, towel in hand, and started wiping down the bar. "Marine, go to the apartment and get some sleep. I'll see you in a bit. Gimme a little suga." Babe stood leaning across the bar and gently kissed her lips. Her face took on a shimmery glow, "And just that quick, all this girl can think of is climbing your body. There's something special about you, Babe Vicarelli." With a sexy wink, he smiled and walked away, turning at the door; he double-thumped his fist over his heart. "You too," she mouthed, "See you at home."

Trinity's place always had an infused relaxing scent like from the beach; not knowing the actual name of the oil, it reminded him of the coast, which then triggered memories of the conversation with Chop. He grabbed a bottle of water and chugged it down, his mind racing with flashes of that entire day. It had all been strange, the whole setup. Is that what it was, a setup? Did Chop want him to see the dead guy, find Hadley drugged out, and then link all the possibilities of a drug business? And if so, to what avail? What was the point? His mind whirled around in a dizzying tornadic explosion of what-ifs, but nothing made sense. He flipped the flashes to remembrances of Trinity's dad. What was that conversation about, and what was the purpose? It was like he'd embarked on a train to crazytown. To think all this bullshit happened in the space of a couple of days. Hard as he tried, he couldn't stop the kaleidoscope of thoughts shifting in his brain. Was this merry-go-round ever going to end?

Stripping off his clothes and turning on the shower, Babe waited for the water to heat up. His phone started buzzing on the marble vanity. He wrapped a towel around himself; there was something not right about answering a call naked—it was unnatural. A crooked grin came to his face, hearing in the recoils of his mind Trinity teasing him about getting on the phone with her dad and the need to be clothed. Whatever he did was in private; he was that kind of guy. His kisses to Trinity in public were barely a peck, never sucking the breath out of her or rubbing himself all over her; however, Babe suspected sexy Miss Trinity would have no objection. He liked their dichotomy; it made things interesting. She kept him on his toes, especially with her surprise crotch grabs. Babe chuckled, thinking of her audacious gropes; while out of his comfort zone, he thirsted for her spontaneity.

The phone had stopped vibrating, and he waited for the ping of voicemail. The ping never came, so he got in the now steamy shower. Thinking about Trinity so much made him want her in the rawest sense, every nerve ending electrified. Four more hours and she'd be home, and he planned to have her, to consume her tiny body. Chills ran up his spine, and he could feel a tingle from the tips of his toes, causing his heart to pound and his breaths to rapidly heighten, the same way he felt when he torqued the neck of the girl-beater. His feelings were convoluted at best. How could he equate taking life to creating an abundance of pleasure and the thrilling explosion of his passion? With thoughts still bombarding his brain, he finished his shower and began toweling off.

Babe felt the readiness and heat pulsing from his nether regions. He growled like a wild beast as his expulsion shot with powerful bursts into the towel. The phone's vibration robbed him of the residual involuntary shivers and uncontrollable momentary weakness, propelling him into reality and disturbing his perfectly euphoric execution.

The number wasn't familiar. "Vicarelli." He answered pungently.

"Vic, it's Tanger Vallas. Sorry about the time, but I just got the weirdest phone call from Tim Faraday. You remember him, Chop? This is the second time he's called me in the past few weeks."

"I do," he responded in a tone of aggravation.

"He says he needs help; somebody's after him and his old lady. I haven't seen that crazy fuck in two years, and he calls me—first time looking for you." He sounded perplexed.

"And you call me? Why?" Things were getting stranger and stranger.

"He said you're after him; you're that somebody, dude."

Babe stepped into his sleeping pants. "What the fuck? The dude's fucking out of it, strung out on dope, and if I were you, I'd stay as far away from him as possible. Just my opinion, Vallas. He's fuckin nuts. For your sake, stay away from him. I think he's mixed up with a cartel drug operation. Some bad fuckin' people. Whatever you do, don't tell him where you live. Out of the blue, he shows up in New Orleans while I'm having a drink asking me to help him."

Vallas broke in, "Sorry, sir, I told him where you were at. I didn't know he was a fucking loonie at the time. I remembered you said you were from New Orleans and were going back home but had to do something regarding VA. Didn't mean to stir up a hornet's nest."

He grabbed a hand towel and rubbed it against his hair. "I would've probably done the same. Man, we went through hell together. Chop's got some sad sob story. I bit and wished like hell I hadn't, but I felt obliged, ya know. He's not the same man you think he is. Good luck, Vallas."

"He has no idea where I live. He asked, but that's as far as it went before he started begging. Not to be a douche, but I hung up. Not my fuckin' problem; I was curious when he mentioned you, Vic."

"Good. Talk about a train wreck." Babe blew out a hard breath. "Take care, ma brotha, and you're wise to stay clear."

After the phone call, there was no way he was getting to sleep. He dressed and went back to Louie's.

Trinity was jiving in her groove—head bopping, shoulders slightly rolling, and her ass damn near twerking. It was a show, to say the least, and he stood for a good minute enjoying her gyration. The girl was in her own world. With a cock of the hip, she turned and slid a drink down the bar without skipping a beat. Suddenly, she froze and looked up with an expression of fear. Her brows knitted, and panic flashed from her eyes. It looked as though she was about to climb over the bar. Babe moved in fast, "I couldn't sleep, Trinity. Everything's cool, ma girl."

She slapped him with the towel, "Vicarelli, don't you do me that. I like to have a heart attack. What choo mean you can't sleep? Boy, you sleep on command." She stood with a hand on her hip and the damp towel in the other.

He slid onto his bar stool with Gunner prancing all up and down his leg. "Someone's happy to see me, right, boy? I'm gonna take him for a quick walk. What y'all got that's sweet?"

Trinity turned and, with a big smile, answered, "Me!" She batted her eyelashes, then turned from silly to factual, "I don't think we have anything left, but I'll check. I can make you a daiquiri or White Russian. Lemme see what Shep left in the back. You still want ya two finger—"

"No, ma'am. Water will do fine if Shep didn't leave anything. Meanwhile, I'm taking Gunn for a walk." He stood, and the dog glued to his side, everything wiggling and his tail wagging a mile a minute in anticipation of getting out. "C'mon, Gunn." They crossed the street and headed toward the square about five blocks up. There was no point in trying to go to sleep or thinking the night would fade to slumber.

By this time, it was past midnight. "Gunner, some weird shit's going down. I can feel it in my bones that someone's setting me up for something, but I don't have a clue by who, what, or why. I trust you got my six. They walked along the side of Jackson Square and up to the river. A few grunge kids were toking a doobie; one nudged the person next to him, then they went silent, eying Babe.

"Cool dog," one of the kids piped. "What's his name?"

Babe stopped, cocked his head to the side with a brief twitch to the corner of his mouth. "Gunner."

Looking up through a mass of stringy hair, another questioned, "You're the guy that saved those kids? It was totally you. You a cop?"

The boy attached to the joint sputtered, "He's a Marine, dude. Can't ya tell? They all got that same look. He looks like my dad." He looked up at Babe, "Want a toke?" Holding out the doob.

Babe rattled a laugh. "Pass, but you enjoy and be careful, y'all; there's a lot of bad people around. Stick together. Get something to eat." He handed each of the five a few bucks. The kids were stoked and undoubtedly wanted more exchange with the cool big guy. Babe and Gunner started walking, followed by endless questions. If bathed with brushed hair, the girl was cute, and Babe guessed she was probably around fourteen years old. She seemed as chatty as reefer boy.

"We stick together, mister. There's a fuckin'gang jumping loners, an' once they got 'em; we never see 'em again. Cops don't care. Some of the cops are nice enough, but most don't give a hearty shit about us street kids. A lot has been disappearing, an' I mean a lot."

Babe's ears prickled with the thought. Most of the kids, while probably runaways, ran for some reason. They didn't seem like bad apples, but one never knew—probably some shoplifting, petty theft, and a loitering nuisance, bad for business but mostly harmless. They were the perfect example of those needing someone to watch over them. Running through his mind the whole time they spoke was *not mine to do; walk away.*

The group chattered during the rest of the walk; Babe listened to the barrage of absurdity. Kids being kids. As they approached Louie's, Babe spoke. "Y'all be careful; this is my stop."

"Mister, you come here a lot? The man that owns this place is cool; sometimes he gives us food out the back but don't want us hangin' around here." Babe waved his arm as though saying keep on walking and nodded to the group with a one-sided smile.

"Babe, it seems like you collected a bunch of kids along the way. Y'all have a good walk?" Tussling Gunn's fur, he glanced at her with a lopsided grin. "I'm homeward bound, ma man. You comin'?" Trinity asked with an arched brow. She grabbed her backpack and came from behind the bar going for the exit. "It's been a long ass day, hadn't it?"

"Too long," he responded.

She strolled alongside him, "So, I want to know all about the chat with my dad. Also, big guy, I never heard a peep about Pensacola. You gonna make me wait until my day off before I hear the whole story? All's I heard is it was messed up, nothing more, and ma man, that ain't gonna cut it."

They breezed through the lobby and went straight to her apartment. She locked the door and started peeling her tee shirt off. "Trinity, you ever wear anything under your shirt?" Taking off her jeans, she hopped on one foot into her room. He followed, amused as she bounced and grunted, cussin' up a storm.

"These jeans have got to go. They're like so tight on my legs I can hardly get them off. They feel all slick-like. Ughh! What do you mean, like what would I wear under my shirt?" She tipped her head to the side, pointing at him. "If you mean a bra, obviously, you haven't looked too close 'cause this girl's got some little bitty titties and don't need no support. She turned and walked into the bathroom, grabbing the towel by the sink. She looked at the towel and then at him. "Babe, looks like you done had a party before I got home."

"No party, just thinkin' of you. What can I say? There's more where that came from?" He laughed straight from the belly. "And like I said, you got a nice rack. If they were any bigger, you'd look, well, not proportioned. They're perfect." His eyes glossed with laughter tears.

"Oh, you think this is funny? Boy, you better get real busy with me. I see how it is. Yup, you better get me up to speed since I missed half the entertainment." She walked into the shower, washing all the bar grunge off her body. He folded his clothes neatly on the vanity and then got in the shower.

"How's this?" Pointing to his awakened crotch.

"That's a beginning, but only the beginning, hardly the show stopper." He lathered up, rinsed, and then picked her up, carrying her, still wet from the shower, to the bed.

"For my show-stopping performance, you naughty girl," he lowered himself for an up-close and personal encounter. She grabbed his hair as he bathed her in kisses.

"Oh God, Babe," she gasped.

Five a.m. came way too fast, and he felt exhausted. Babe went through his morning routine, but it took everything he had. Even Gunner was slow to get moving and threw a glance at Babe as if to say, "Are you kidding me?"

The morning run to the construction site woke him some; however, he knew he looked like hell, his face drawn and tight, not relaxed from a peaceful night's sleep. A block from the site, he sensed an approaching vehicle and turned in enough time to jump on the hood of a parked car with Gunner in his arms. "You stupid motherfucker!" he bellowed.

A strange sensation overcame him like the driver hadn't drifted into the zone; the near catastrophe was purposeful. He got the first number and last three letters of the Louisiana license plate—four, something, something, H-M-T. It was a black Lexus SUV. He felt more rattled; he guessed it had something to do with the element of surprise. The first thought that came to mind was that he needed to back away from this new lifestyle; he'd lost his edge and gotten sloppy, irresponsible, like a civilian. *Hell no!* He thought.

Upon entering the job site, Glenn called him into the office even though he was on his way there anyway. "Vicarelli, you okay? Even with the TV blaring and the A/C humming, your voice almost shook the trailer."

"Yes, sir. Some stupid cocksucker almost ran us over, my furry pal and me." He sat with Gunner, who rested his head on Babe's knee. Even the dog felt apprehensive. "If it doesn't put you in a trick bag, I'm gonna take next week off." Glenn frowned, wrinkling his forehead with concern, but told Babe to take whatever time he wanted and asked if he wanted an advance on his pay. "No, sir, just time." It was Thursday, which gave him that night and the next day to get things situated in his place and his head for a week's isolation. Thinking it through, he figured Trinity was not going to be as casual about his time away from her; in fact, she'd likely throw a tantrum. His mind churned with thoughts; *Maybe I should ghost her, nixing an explanation. She'd never understand. Better to ask forgiveness afterward than create a situation before.*

LOST AND FOUND

*A*fter work, Babe walked to his truck and headed toward Carrollton to the new giant grocery store. He bought a week's worth of bottled water, orange juice, eggs, bread, and a variety of meat. He started to buy a bottle of scotch but passed on the thought. For this exercise, he needed to be of sound mind and body; he knew it would be brutal, and some of his demons undoubtedly would show. It would have to be like preparing for a mission—no sex, no drinking, pure reflection, and immersion.

Babe filled the fridge and seemed to have enough food for a week. After jumping in the shower and getting the construction dirt off him, he dressed and headed for Louie's with Gunner. His furry pal would have to stay with Trinity for the week. This whole detox of civilian life would need to be solo—his heart screamed to his soul that Trinity needed to know, and either she loved him enough to let him go, or she wasn't the one for him, and the sooner they knew it, the better. The internal debate continued until he and Gunner reached Louie's.

Trinity was full-stride behind the bar, hustling up a bevy of drinks. Customers lined up all along the bar and three deep in spots. Finn was pouring, and he surmised Shep had called in more help because there were faces bussing that he didn't recognize. Finn and Trinity made an excellent tag team. The conversation would have to take place after she got off. She spied him upon entry and had a reserved sign in front of his seat, which he found hilarious; nonetheless, he was grateful. No doubt, the little lady ignited him, and there was something special about their relationship. He only hoped those feelings would remain once he disclosed that he would be checking out for a week, maybe two. Babe hoped he wasn't going down a hole he couldn't climb out of because that was always a possibility he didn't want to confront. *PTSD, my ass,* he thought, *but what if the shrinks were right? And then again, this is precisely why time alone is needed—to get my shit together.* For all he knew, there truly was someone out to get him, and it wasn't a paranoid delusion.

Trinity quickly slid his drink to him, and one of the new bussers placed some skins in front of him. He looked at Trinity with questioning eyes and a slight tilt of his head. She blew him a kiss and sparked a smile meant only for him. Babe drew a deep breath, filling his lungs, then slowly and silently exhaled. The crowd overwhelmed him, raising the question, was he struggling with PTSD? He'd researched, and some of the feelings he was experiencing might be classic, according to Dr. Google—delusion, paranoia, perhaps anxiety, or depression. The crowd had made him uncomfortable, but he wasn't anxious, didn't feel depressed, and certainly had no thoughts of offing himself. Actually, he just needed to put a whetstone to his senses; they'd dulled. After a half hour, most of the guests moved away from the bar en masse as though on cue and took up residence at the far end of Louie's, the table area where folks could sit and eat. Tour group? Too old to be fraternity crap, maybe reunion.

One couple from the group remained at the bar—a sizeable man, probably six-two or three, well-built with a striking redhead almost glued to his side. The man looked vaguely familiar, but Babe couldn't place him. He'd get an occasional profile of the man, but other than that, it was the back of his head as his date consumed his attention. Despite doing nothing improper, the couple radiated red-hot heat. Their vibes were palpable to anyone watching. Trinity said something to the man, and the couple began to make their way to Babe.

The man possessed confidence with a warm demeanor. He walked up to Babe and stretched out his hand. "I'm sure you don't remember me as it was a nerve-racking night, at best, but I'm Mike Landry, a friend of

Trinity's family." The light bulb went off in Babe's mind, and he nodded with a thankful smile. Mike Landry was the plastic surgeon that took care of Trinity the night she was abducted, beaten, and raped by her ex-brother-in-law. "This is my wife, Rainie."

The woman had dark auburn hair and the lightest eyes he'd ever seen; she was exotic, with a raspy voice. "Nice to meet you, and thank you for your service. I understand you were in the military, and did I understand right, your name is Babe?" She had a sparkling smile that emanated from her whole being. They made a most handsome couple.

"Yes, ma'am. Babe Vicarelli is my name. As far as service, it was mine to do." He returned her smile and looked at the doctor. "It is good to see you under different circumstances, sir."

Rainie cut in, "Unfortunately, we are at this surgeon's conference," she rolled her eyes; "Otherwise, I'd want to visit for a while. The military has always intrigued me. Wow, I mean, intense, I bet." Her husband took her hand, and she squinted with a glare at him, "Michael, I'm coming, Jeez Louise. Sorry, Babe, and by the way, what a cool-ass name. I hope we run into each other again. My friend, Mer has a brother that—"

"Rainie, say good night." She laughed with a sound that came from her soul.

"Good night, y'all." Babe closed his eyes with a snicker and thought what a handful she must be for the good doc.

The brief conversation conjured the fear from that night, jumping into the discussion with Trinity's dad. One thing was for sure, Antoine Noelle spoke his mind without hesitation, asking Babe about offing the guy and did he have a problem doing it. *Did he have a problem ridding the world of that useless piece of shit? Hell, no.* He only wished he could've tortured him as a repayment for what he did to his lady—*sick bastard.* No matter what, he wouldn't be muscle for hire or someone's beck-and-call assassin.

With a slight break at the bar, Trinity moved fast to his end. "You were later than usual tonight. Hell, with the crowd, it was probably a good thing. Did you recognize Dr. Landry? Ooh, I had a major crush on him when I was younger, before Rainie and their five kids. She's a kick in the ass. Crazy, boisterous, and frank as can be." She glanced from his eyes to his lips the whole time she spoke to him. He could tell she wanted him. "We'll have to meet up with them some night; actually, I think Bethany planned a barbeque sometime soon. I bet they'll be invited. You remember my sister Bethany?"

"How could I forget? Yes, ma'am. I like your sister; in fact, I've found everyone in your family interesting." He glanced over the top of his tumbler at her.

She cupped the sides of her mouth with her hands, "And my dad? Is he interesting?" She giggled like a teenager.

Babe cleared his throat and raised his glass to his lips, staring intently at her. *How to answer this, hm.* "We have a vital thing in common—you." He winked his right eye at her with a curious smirk. Some things were best left unsaid. What would one say? Oh, by the way, did you know your dad is part of the Mob? Probably somewhere in the recesses of her mind, she knew, but most people didn't want to think poorly of their parents; that was most people. He knew who his parents were from a very early age. His mom died while he was in Afghanistan, and to hell with his father; he hadn't seen him for years and didn't plan on it anytime in the future, and that was if he was still breathing. As the expression said, his father was dead to him, sad but true.

From time to time, he wondered about his mom when he went off to college and then the service. Babe would stop and see her every few years, but they never spoke of the past. There had to be some normalcy at one point in time, but with all family gone, other than the mysterious older brother he'd never met, his early years were blank, not even faint memories, fucking blank. Perhaps no memories were better than tortuous nightmares.

The crowd didn't appear to be leaving soon, so after about an hour and some food; he bid goodnight. "Trinity, wake me up when you get in; it's important."

50

She tipped her head toward her left shoulder, trying to size him up. "Big man, everything okay?"

"Sure thing, but make sure I wake up fully," he took on a devilish naughty grin, "And I'm not talking about you coming in and jumping my bones." She laughed and blew him a kiss.

The one thing about being in the service is most everything was orderly with no grey areas, purely black and white. Superiors gave orders, and Babe obeyed, pure and simple. In a firefight, the objective was clear: to stay alive, keep his team alive, and either eliminate the threat or capture his assignment. Civilian life was a crap shoot. There were no clear-cut answers, and every day revealed more challenges. He developed somewhat of a routine with his morning ritual, going to work, then Louie's, and ending with sleep, whether his place or hers, but mostly hers. The tricky part came with the human interaction interspersed in the factors of each day. When it came down to it, and all the trimmings and facades were stripped away, people were primal beings. Darwin summed it up perfectly in his hypothesis life was all about survival of the fittest. He'd studied the Darwinian evolutionary theory, and to fully live by his deducements, Babe needed to reproduce, creating more specimens like him. The question remained, though, was he a good guy or a bad guy?

Had he known for certain he was a good guy, to spawn more like him would make the world a better place, but if he was a sociopath and an evil man, he sure as shit didn't want to create more monsters to inhabit the earth. Evil was manifesting faster and faster with each new generation. Sin, as Trinity referred to almost everything that wasn't sunshine and roses, was running rampant. His solitude might cleave the bad, and he could eradicate it once and for all. Facing his demons would be the only way to become whole, maybe.

"Babe, wake up." The slight touch of her hand put him on alert, and his body flinched. "Shh, you told me to wake you when I got home." He sat up, stretched, and wiped the sand from his eyes. She turned on the bedside lamp. "I'm getting in the shower, I'll be quick, and then we can talk, but I'm funk nasty right now." He took her hand and pulled her to him for a sweet hello kiss.

"Take your shower; I'm gonna grab some water and be right back." She nodded but had a distinct curiosity in her gaze. He had her attention, and it wasn't as he feared. She was ready to listen. Babe brought two bottles of water back into the bedroom, and she was already toweling off.

Trinity sat cross-legged on the bed and turned toward him. With concentration written all over her expression, she asked. "What's up, my sweet man?" Love and compassion exuded from her. There was no doubt she loved him.

Babe cleared his throat to get rid of the sleep in his mouth. "Hear me out and hold your questions, okay?"

"Okay," she dubiously answered.

"I've been going through some weirdness and feel like I'm losing my edge. It's not good for anyone. I need to re-group, ya know, get my shit together. I'm struggling, really having a hard time. When I went to Pensacola, I found Chop's wife, not at home, but in some foul double wide, nasty. The place was a dump, trash strewn all over with drugs and the paraphernalia that goes along with it. A dead man, probably overdosed, was lying across the bed, and she was huddled, barely alive, in the corner of a disgusting closet. Didn't look like the girl I remembered. It pissed me off, but I called nine-one-one and left after calling Chop, the lying piece of shit. Anyway, you were right; he's running drugs for, I'm guessing, a cartel because he said he couldn't get out of the situation. I call bullshit on that, but I know it won't be easy, and they'll likely run him down and eliminate the possibility of exposure. He's a grown-ass man and got greedy, and that's what happens when greed takes over. He shoulda just done tours or gotten a construction job like I did."

Trinity sat quietly and listened. He could tell she wanted to talk but didn't. "Then, your dad wants to talk to me. He owns the construction company where I work, which I didn't know, and he offers me a chance to move up the ladder, so to speak. Trinity, your father loves y'all and is doing the best he can to provide. I think he wanted me to join the business, maybe, but don't get me wrong; I'm not being all self-righteous—I'm not for sale." She leaned into him but put her hand over her lips and listened, desperately wanting to say something. My nightmares and hallucinations have slowed, and I know this will sound delusional, but I think someone is trying to kill me. I've got to sort my head a bit without distraction. I'm leaving Gunner with you for a week and going into isolation. I've got to get it together, my girl. I'm not leaving, and I hope you'll still want me after a week or two.

"I almost forgot; your dad wanted to know my intentions. Was I planning on marrying you?" She rolled her eyes and brought her hand to her lips in surprise or embarrassment. "I predicted you would feel it was rushing things, but I told him I loved you, and you were the first woman I ever loved. My love for you, Trinity, is for keeps, but I gotta get my head together. I'm not ready to be a civilian; not sure what I'm meant to be, but Mr. Regular Stiff, ain't it." He exhaled audibly as though his confession had lifted a massive weight from his chest. He blinked a few times, waiting for Trinity to break the silence. It felt like an eternity. Silence.

"Of course, Gunn can stay with me, and I'll take care of him. Babe, I love you, you know that, shit everyone in Louie's knows. I understand the need to be isolated, left alone to work through whatever it is that's going on. I get it, but I gotta say I worry that you'll go to some dark place and never come back." Tears slowly trickled from her eyes. "That scares the crap outta me. I've heard that what you're going through is common, and I know the statistics. After the first episode I witnessed, I did a lot of research. While you don't think you have PTSD, I'm not so sure." She looked down at her hands entwined in her lap. "I'll do whatever you ask, but promise me that if you start to do something you can't come back from, you'll call me." He tipped his head to the side like Gunner often did when they made a squeaky noise, somewhat confused. "Like eat your gun." Babe nodded to affirm that he understood what she meant.

They sat still, looking into each other's eyes, trying to connect and heal their souls. In a coarse whisper, he asked, "Will you be alright?"

She nodded, "Babe, I can't say I understand or have any comprehension of what you did while you were over there, but I know it was brutal and had to leave some scars behind. They'll never be gone for good, but with time you can heal." She looked away, and he could tell she was weighing her next words, but finally, she looked back into his eyes and spoke. "Trey stopped by for a chat and started asking me all kinds of weird questions about you. He asked if I had ever talked to you about God and church. Trey wanted to know how much I knew about you and did I think you were a good man or a monster. Babe, I know you, and even though you have your moments where I probably should be scared as hell of you, I'm not. You've told me about the previous owner of Gunner and about that night of horrors, but I also think it frequently happens, more than you admit to me. I don't look at you and think killer, maybe I should, but I don't. I didn't tell Trey because I know you'd never hurt an innocent person or a child. You got a tough exterior, but right here," she poked his chest, "is a frightened little boy that became a real-life superhero, and that's how I look at you." He cleared his throat a few times, and this time he looked away. She could see a gloss over his eyes but knew he'd fight the tear from falling. That would make him completely vulnerable. "Let me hold you, please, and it's okay if a tear or two drops; it doesn't make you any less of a man or a Marine."

Babe stiffened, "I know that." He spread his arms, and she crawled into his lap. She held on to him as though it were a matter of life and death. He allowed the embrace and gave in to the tears he'd held back for so long. "I love you," he choked out. "Will you marry me one day and have children with me, or are you afraid they'd be like me?"

Trinity pulled away, breaking their embrace, and stared into his eyes. "One day, I don't know when, but I will marry you and be thrilled to have little Babes. You're not your father, nor am I my father, and we will be great parents. We gotta first get you through this shit. Take however long you need, and I'll be right by your side when you make your way through, but first, promise me you'll call if you get into that dark hole. Also, Babe, you are never alone, God is always with you, but that's a long talk for another time. Can we sleep in each other's arms? Maybe skip your morning workout and sleep just a tiny bit longer. He laid back in the bed, pulling her to him, and she curled into his arm with the peacefulness of a silent night.

ENCOUNTERS IN HELL

*A*s planned, Friday, when he knocked off work, he went straight to the tiny apartment with all the supplies to last for a week. Stripping his clothes, he got into the shower. *I'm ready for whatever you sling my way. Get out of my head, you motherfuckers!* The beating spray pounded his neck and back. A whirlwind of thoughts raced through his head, wearing a path of hot coals throughout his abdomen, like the most intense workout ever, but without that worked muscle feel-good. There wasn't a blast of endorphins, more like a fearful running for his life. He waited to see if the voices would start up or if any of his ghosts would show. He was ready for battle. He shook his head like a dog after a bath, streaking the shower glass with a barrage of flying droplets. It had been a few months since his last haircut, and Trinity had commented that she liked his hair longer. *Hmm, don't know 'bout that.* He ran his hands through his hair and toweled off.

Babe padded his way into the living room, the walls adorned with military posters, his service flag, and framed team pictures from some of his assignments. He discarded the towel, being more vulnerable in his nakedness, then set the stage. He took the photos from around the room and surrounded himself with the memories.

"Let's get this show on; I'm waiting and ready. If You are real, Trinity's God, give me the strength I need to fight my demons. Save me from me."

He heard sounds that seemed to be coming from the bedroom, and the hallucination would start any second. He knew it wasn't real, but damn, it felt all too authentic. He waited for hours, but nothing; the slight noise had been all the activity and didn't develop into the screaming cries, the sound of gunfire, or the heavy smell of smoke. For all he knew, it could have been the soap sliding out the tray onto the shower floor. He knew this was something he had to do, but he missed Trinity, and it hadn't even been twenty-four hours. When eleven hit, he climbed into bed. The demons would come, he knew it, so getting sleep might be for the best.

Every time the episodes occurred, he relived the same nightmares over and over, including sights, smells, sounds, trepidation, and hyper-awareness. The sweat would run profusely, coating his body like a foamed neoprene dive suit. Babe drifted to sleep.

The morning came with an uneventful night. He put on some short-legged boxer briefs, which stretched to maximum capacity. Like any other day, he began the morning routine. The day progressed, and the demons stayed hidden. Babe spent his time researching the residual effects of psychological and physical abuse, switching to his supposed older brother. Ancestry sent updates as they discovered more facts of interest matching his DNA. He opened the latest email, and as he began to read, he noticed a rumbling noise coming from his bedroom at the back of the apartment. As he turned toward the hallway, a familiar scent lingered in the air; he knew hell was opening up.

Dense smoke hazed from the hall as though it was real. The unit ducking beneath the rhythmic thudding of the rotor blades ran from the helo. The whipped-up plume, pungent with the smell of animal shit, created a dust layer of a most repulsive nature; they hauled ass in a staggered line advancing the ridge. He could smell remnants of a smoldering fire, caustic fumes trying to camouflage and distract their senses, yet there was an eery calm like some eternal hangtime—every nerve ending on high alert. He looked back and saw Malloy, Brewster, Vallas, Hurley, Kellogg, Trapini, and Jackson. They were looking to him for advancement.

The mission was clear, search and eliminate Taliban snipers along Death Pass without getting slaughtered in an ambush. The quiet and stillness were unsettling, knowing hell could let loose at any moment without notice. Any man or woman that said they were without apprehension or fear was lying through their teeth. They listened for the slightest snap of a twig or tumble from loose rock. This was Taliban terrain, and they knew it better than anyone, making Babe and his unit a step behind. His jaws throbbed as he clenched his teeth in consternation. It was like being on a high cliff preparing to jump off into a frothing sea—hit the deep spot or fracture into a thousand pieces atop the rocks below? Slaughter or be slaughtered?

Crouched down, he cautiously stepped backward, nestling behind low cover, no idea where his unit had found shielding—his eyes in constant scan and dart mode. He heard a whisper, not one of his Marines, but it was near impossible to know where it originated.

A loud crash that sounded like shattering glass and a hard slam of something big drew his attention. Before him, he could see his mother lying on her stomach, a gash above her eyebrow with streaks of blood, and her eyes lasering straight to his, "Get in the closet, son, now." This hallucination was a brand new experience that tore at his heart's very essence. *It took him far back in time to when he was ten years old, and the cover he hid behind was his father's oversized padded recliner, not a rugged outgrowth along a ridge over Death Pass. He scampered in his mind to the back of a closet and could hear her screams and his father's abusive beratement, complete with thudding blows and piercing slaps.*

Anna Johansen was a beautiful Norwegian girl on holiday with her parents to America. On the family's stop in New Orleans, seventeen-year-old Anna fell for the dreamy-eyed Italian, Gino Vicarelli, 25, in nineteen seventy-four. Anna was elegant and statuesque at five-foot-eleven. Her flowing snowy blonde hair, big blue eyes, and unique accent mesmerized Gino, and the two fell madly in love.

As it was nearing her eighteenth birthday with pre-university schooling complete, Anna begged her parents to allow Gino to join them on their travel west to Las Vegas, Los Angeles, and up along the coast to Oregon and Washington. While in Las Vegas, she and Gino married at the well-known, *A Little White Wedding Chapel*, with her parent's reluctant permission. After visiting the sights in Oregon and Washington, they returned to New Orleans. Anna's parents were heartbroken and hesitant but returned to their home in Narvik.

Things were the picture of paradise for one year, and Anna stayed in contact with regular calls to her mother and father. When she learned of an unexpected pregnancy, Gino blamed her. Life in New Orleans turned horrific with his verbal and emotional abuse refusing to let her phone her parents in Norway; she was alone and miserable. Anna's parents, Rune and Astrid Johansen, found it unsettling that Anna's calls ended abruptly. Their concern was so great that they uprooted and moved to New Orleans to live. Fortunately, they had affluence, and the move wouldn't cause hardship. After several weeks of searching, they found and showered her with love. Rune was a big man, towering at six-foot-five; he discreetly threatened Gino regarding his practices with their daughter. Her father's intimidation merely served to amp up the abuse turning it more physical. When bruises appeared on his daughter's arms, Rune approached Gino at the neighborhood tavern while Astrid took Anna and her belongings to their house on Chestnut Street to live. Shortly thereafter, Anna delivered a boy; her father named him Mays after the great American baseball player Willie Mays. From all appearances, Mays favored his mother's family with blond hair and blue eyes. At the rate he grew, the pediatrician's opinion was that Mays would carry on his Viking ancestry and be a giant of a man like his grandfather, Rune.

Because the heart wants what the heart wants, it took no time for Gino to work his way back to Anna, promising never to put his hands on her again. Their lives looked like most marriages for the next four years, with slight ups and downs but mostly happy. Astrid forgave her son-in-law and attributed his behavior to his youth and perhaps his upbringing. They hadn't met his parents or heard him speak of them. Water under the bridge, so it seemed, but Rune did not forgive and stayed silent. He was active in the boy's life while Gino worked and frequented bars. The suave Italian slid into alcoholism, and the abuse began again. By this time, Mays was in kindergarten. The faculty started noticing the bruises on Mays and witnessing Anna's submissive behavior, they reported the situation, and the state placed him in foster care. Gino gave up his paternity rights and signed him over to an anonymous adoptive family who quickly moved to another part of the state. Rune and Astrid were devastated but felt it would be best for all concerned. They had contemplated taking the boy, but then Gino would always be in the picture, so they advised Anna not to fight the issue.

Five years passed, and Anna found herself with child once more. Gino mended his ways and weaseled into Anna's good graces again. Things would be different this time; she felt with a heart full of hope. It wasn't long before another son was born. While Anna filled out paperwork at the hospital, her father visited with a gift of roses and chocolates. While he held his dark-haired grandson, he said, "Anna, his name shall be Babe; what a lovely name for this fine baby boy. Babe Ruth like the best baseball player of all time. I suppose he'll have to have his father's last name, but Babe Ruth Vicarelli makes for a nice name, no?" His eyes twinkled as he gazed upon his daughter.

"It's a fine name, Papa, but I think we shall name him Babe Rune Vicarelli. I can tell Papa he will be fierce and strong like you since you are his Farfar. She sighed deeply. "Part of me wishes we could go back to Narvik. Bring Babe and teach him the ancient ways of his people. His destiny should be of great power and a life of abundance, not like—"

At that moment, Gino arrogantly strutted into the room, arms wildly expressive. "You think I'm going to let you move to Norway? You must be out of your fuckin' mind. I stood by the door and heard your scheming, you bitch." Rune stood and handed the baby back to Anna.

Towering over Gino, he placed his right hand on the back of his son-in-law's neck and squeezed. "You'll not speak to my daughter in such a manner. I will squash you under my foot, you Italian dog. Anna, do not go home to this wretch of a man."

Gino puffed out his chest, "Listen, you son-of-a-bitch, you are in my country. So keep your fuckin nose out of my family's affairs, or get the fuck out of America. You don't scare me; I have my paisans; it's you who should be afraid." He formed his hand into the shape of a gun, acting like he pulled the trigger of an invisible weapon.

The baby began to cry. "Stop this, now." That was the last time Anna spoke to Gino in a scolding tone. She would go to her parent's home for days at a time, and Babe grew with love from his grandparents and watched as his mother became weaker and more timid. His father had beaten her down and taken all the will from her heart.

The disturbing sight continued; he could feel a tightness in his chest with pounding aches of dread. Babe cupped his hands over his ears, sobbing real tears from so long ago. *His illusory image yelled, "No, you sick bastard." He was no longer the frightened ten-year-old; he witnessed his twelve-year-old self grab the kitchen chair by one of the legs and rage as he pummeled his father until the chair was in broken pieces scattered about the room. He saw his old man, blood running from his mouth and nose, crying with howling wails as his arm dangled from his body. The shoulder, no longer squared, drooped mercilessly. Debris from the chair stuck between furniture as it lay where it landed. "You will never hurt anyone again, you sick bastard."* The hallucination, while frightening, was also necessary, and as it disappeared, Babe stood tall and beat his fists on his chest with a loud bellow. *One monster put to rest*, he thought.

The next thing he knew, *his hallucination plummeted to the police banging on his parent's front door, "NOPD."* He had no reason to fear the *police, so he quietly opened the door and let them inside. The first officer spoke, "What the hell? Boy, are you okay?" Babe answered yes, noticing the blood sprayed on his clothes.*

His father, still yelping and crying, spewed hostility, "He's fuckin' crazy. The boy's insane; he started beating me with the chair for no reason. I wasn't doing a damn thing. He went berserk."

Without anger or remorse, he responded, "That's a lie." He heard the echo of his voice bounce off the walls of the room. An ambulance took his father somewhere, and the men put him in the police car and brought him to the station. Vision fizzled.

The childhood hallucination was a first, but maybe that's where his violence and darkness began. It was no wonder he had an absence of emotion. His father had tortured it out of him. His body, drenched in sweat, glistened. He swallowed down two bottles of water, grabbed a towel, and began back on the computer. On the screen was the last thing he'd pulled up—Mays Connolly, 46, an attorney from Atlanta, Georgia. *How many people are named Mays? Forty-six? Was this too coincidental? Do I even want to know more? Not now.* Clasping his hands behind his head, he rocked back and closed his eyes. His mind jetted to a most familiar and disturbing scene, thrusting him to combat, reliving the operation in a snap. He tightly clamped his hands to the chair, holding on for dear life with his heart racing an Indy five hundred.

Crouched to his left, he saw Cummings, signaling he had a sniper in his sights. Babe put his fist up for him to remain still, scanning around for other snipers within their proximity. His eyes focused like a hawk. He felt the adrenalin soar in his body as he signaled to take the shot. No sooner did he shoot the sniper than a rash of bullets ripped through Cummings, leaving pieces of him among the surrounding rocky terrain. Babe had seen where the flurry originated, and he and Kellogg both hummed grenades behind a cluster of rocks forming a natural barrier. Two shattering explosions created a mass of carnage and a gruesome scene of their success. Their strike allowed them to advance.

Babe could hear the rumbling of feet. Was it approaching or retreating?

It was difficult to distinguish. More firepower commenced, and he knew some of his Marines were in a deadly firefight, but he couldn't find them due to the smoky haze and dust clouds. He felt the immense responsibility of ensuring his men returned while completing the assignment, and he'd already lost one. He saw himself advancing toward Vallas, who was leaning over Trapini. Vallas squared eyes with Babe and passed his hand under his chin. Fuck, another gone, which tripped him into even deeper determination. He signaled for Vallas to fan out along with Hurley, Kellogg, and Brewster. Malloy and Jackson had their backs. He detected movement, and they all opened fire. When the madness stopped, silence returned; it was the silence of death. In a staggered formation, the unit cautiously treaded along the Pass with an occasional single shot fired.

Babe had Trapini's dead body heaved over his shoulder; he glanced down at the dead Marine's face. The looping hallucination, as always, evolved into Trapini looking at Babe and saying, "Why me? Why me, Cap?" He'd heard those words too many times. At that moment, he wanted the misery to end. Indeed, why did he make it? The scene faded, and he dropped his head into his hands; he found himself sitting in the corner with his arms resting on his knees, no longer at the computer. The heaviness in his body made every muscle ache, hitching his breaths as though he had ended a wrestling match with a monstrous opponent. Babe walked to the circle of pictures and picked up the photo of the unit that took down one group of snipers along the Pass. They had been fierce, and while they lost a couple of excellent Marines, the rest came back intact, but as always, each of them left a piece of their soul in the craggy, dusty hell.

He tapped the smiling faces of Cummings and Trapini, clearing his throat, "Y'all were fierce. I failed you." Fatigued, he lay back on the floor, surrounded by his memories and nightmare experiences, and drifted to sleep. The big man woke in cold sweats, unaware of time and still feeling vulnerable and unsteady. He fixed his concoction of raw eggs and juice, guzzled a couple of water bottles, and began his morning workout, still having no concept of time. *Is it morning? Don't know. Don't care.*

Amidst a pull-up, he heard, *"Vicarelli!"* as though the person was beside him.

He immediately stopped and shouted back with the same intensity, "Yes, sir," and stood rigidly at attention, heart pounding as the blood raced through his body. Tingles ran down his arms straight to his fingertips.

"Follow me." Although standing still, *he watched as his illusory image followed The Commander. "We have a situation whereby we need one devil dog to infiltrate and eliminate without a trace linking to U.S. forces, and you're that one. If seized, you're on your own. This operation is need-to-know, and only you and I are in the know." The Commander showed a picture of an American serviceman.*

"Sir?" Babe questioned, totally flummoxed.

"That's all you need to know. You have your orders, Vicarelli."

"Yes, sir," and they parted ways. The face in the picture was familiar; he remembered that but couldn't pull the detail to mind. Everything changed as he resumed reality, standing in his hallway. This ordeal he had ignited was perhaps the most bizarre and chopped-up experience he'd ever had, but it was of his making. He called the demons, and they showed up, one at a time and in whatever nonsensical order they chose. This was going to be a long week.

He continued his workout, skipping to free weights. His mind reeled, trying to remember the picture he saw and identify the face. The thought hammered his brain with no luck. Perhaps it was something his mind blocked. Why would his commander order him to kill one of their own? Maybe the person had infiltrated their base and assumed someone else's identity or turned thus a sleeper threat. The Commander didn't owe him an explanation; he gave the order, and that was that. Afghanistan was a disaster, and the more it went on, with the new powers in control, the worse it got. Babe thought, *bunch of spineless pussies, without two brain cells to rub together. What the fuck was going on with the leaders?* Troops moved in and out of the base in a perpetual stream. Being a lone wolf, so to speak, he kept to himself; therefore, he wouldn't have necessarily crossed the path of his target, yet, the image had familiarity. The lack of continuity and organization made the U.S. look weak. It had become a different beast since the year he joined.

Babe hit the weights one more time before jumping in the shower. The hot water beat on his back, and he stood still while his mind flipped through the faces of Marines he remembered, but he couldn't find the individual he wanted. The steam in the shower wafted in clouds as he circulated the air with his body movements. Babe thought he heard something and wiped a circle of fog from the shower door. *Looking in from the other side was the face he'd been searching for in his memory—Lee Yuhn. The man stood with his head cocked to his shoulder, buzzed black hair, lifeless brown eyes, and a bloody slice across his throat that had stained the front of his shirt.*

He let the steam start to fog in the window he'd created. Lee Yuhn was from Cincinnati and played a mean game of chess. They'd had a few matches and were on par with each other as far as the strategizing required with chess. Yuhn was an outstanding opponent; it was something he enjoyed. Slowly he recalled the memory and saw Yuhn setting up for a match; Babe had arrived early and silently came up behind the small man, cupping a hand over his mouth and just as quickly drew his blade across the man's throat, then sat him in front of the board. Yuhn was always the one to want and locate an isolated area, which was few and far between, but for this purpose, it served well; there was no evidence that it had been Babe. With a one-sided grin, he thought, *so, this was the traitor or infiltrator.* Babe never suspected; maybe the Commander was sharper than he'd given the man credit, or might there have been an ulterior motive. His big question was why he didn't remember the face; maybe a blocked memory. He followed the order, but at the time, and even at that moment, it still didn't feel right.

After the steamy shower, he padded back to the kitchen in snuggly fitting boxer briefs. Trinity had bought them for him; going commando or cotton boxers was fine with him, but since she liked him in them, it became standard to his daily attire. They stretched tightly around his thighs, but if that blew her skirt up, so be it. Gnawing grumbles tromped inside his belly as he prepared meat and potatoes. Quickly scarfing his food, he returned to his computer staring at the image of what may or may not be his older brother. Thoughts rolled through his mind—wondering what he was like. *Do I really want to rip that wound open for the man; it had to be traumatic.* The more he considered things, the more his curiosity was aroused.

His grandfather thought America and anything American-related was grand. He was borderline obsessed with baseball, hence named his grandsons after baseball legends—Mays after the all-time great Willie Mays and Babe Ruth, and yes, everyone knew The Babe's real name was George, but that wasn't how his grandfather viewed it. If he could emulate anyone, it would have been his mother's father, but the deck wasn't stacked that way. For a moment, he wondered if Gino Vicarelli were still alive, that would be one piece of shit he'd take pleasure in offing, but that wasn't his calling. He wasn't the avenger for personal retribution or retaliation; the man definitely fucked his head up badly. After the hallucination from childhood, Babe felt fairly certain that if he did have PTSD, it was from childhood, not the military or missions.

He returned to the computer. Looking at the picture of the man, he could see his mother's likeness. He wondered how much he might have in common with Mays. Would they be polar opposites or similar? He began researching, finding out anything he could about Mays Connolly. He had graduated from L.S.U. Law School and was a partner in what appeared to be a substantial firm, one with five partners, no telling how many junior partners. *Funny,* he thought; *he has a one-cocked smile, hm.* Nothing else appeared similar. How'd he end up in Georgia?

The man had a rounder face, big light-colored eyes, and a more prominent nose, but their mouths were the same, medium to full lips, nothing like Trinity's puckers. He suspected they were probably about the same size in stature from his features, but he appeared perhaps heavier. After all, if this was his brother, he was ten years older, and maybe ten years from then, he might have some pudge. The Google articles portrayed an astute litigator with some heavy-duty cases to his acclaim—from the comments quoting him, he seemed like a reasonable person.

Rather than complicate issues right then, he needed to hone in on the probability that someone was trying to kill him. Paranoia, perhaps, was one of the things on a long list of possible symptoms of PTSD. It wasn't clearly defined, merely described, and there were many varied descriptions. Loner, check; nightmares, check; hallucinations, sensory inaccuracies, and exaggerations; triple check.

The more he theorized about the guy getting shot and the vehicle attempting to run him down, the more he started putting the pieces together. He grabbed a pad and pen.

1. Chop showing up, and the bullshit drug stuff with a strung-out wife—no doubt, cartel-related. Missing street kids, Chop? *Dead motherfucker if he was responsible.*

2. Something to do with Trinity's dad? *Probably not.* Antoine had been direct in his communication. Babe wasn't a threat to his business or indulgences. He was just the guy that dated the man's daughter.

3. Special Ops covert need to know assignment with him being the target? *Distinct possibility, but far too sloppy and not a marksman, for sure. Nope.*

Hm, he thought, *food for thought.* Maybe flush the person or persons tracking him. Bring it all out in the open. His fingers began to tingle, and his gut was like an itch he couldn't scratch. There was a flurry of possibilities running rampant. He stopped the ponderance and hit the weight bench. There were still dragons he needed to slay.

Babe loaded up three hundred pounds for reps and pushed to exhaustion, but it wasn't enough; he loaded another fifteen. After several lifts, his arms quivered, and he dropped the weight with a loud, primal rumble from the innermost part of his stomach. He needed to run, his adrenalin whipping up with a hurricane force. There were too many moving parts to be stationary and cooped. He figured if someone were out to get him, they'd have his place under surveillance, maybe even his truck; then it hit him. There was still the fully furnished house on Chestnut, bingo! There wasn't a soul who knew about the place; he'd have to take precautions to ensure nobody tailed him.

He grumbled, "Fucking Chop. It's the fucking cartel." Those bastards didn't mess around, similar in many ways to the brutality and derangement of radical Islamists. Was he strictly with the drugs, or was there any relevance to missing street kids and Chop's presence? "Fuck!" Then a nightmare thought crept upon him, *was he the person intending to traffic Trinity?* Instinctually Babe balled his fists and felt the red-hot fire of rage pulse through his body. First things first, get out of his place and to Chestnut Street, then find Chop, bring him to the house, and force the answers out of him. If he were part of the Trinity equation, the consequence would be brutal and unforgiving.

DEMONS

There was no doubt that he was battling inner and roaming demons. Babe was equipped for the ones lurking around; the demons in his head were a different threat altogether. He felt solid in his suspicions of Chop. "Fucking Tim Faraday. He's gonna wish he was never born."

Babe focused on the words of his commander from MARSOC Raider Training. *"Remember the strength of the pack is the wolf, and to coin Rudyard Kipling, The strength of the wolf is the pack. Get what I'm saying? Sometimes, Vicarelli, you'll be the lone wolf; other times, your Marines will look to you for the answers and war as a team. Son, you're one of the best, and you'll do your country proud. Spiritus Invictus, Unconquerable Spirit. You're the type of warrior that births legends. God Speed, Captain."*

"Aye, sir." He wanted to make a difference and be that warrior that could stand alone and win as well as command a team to battle with synchrony and masterpiece precision. He felt the same surge of confidence he had in that conversation. His breath and heart swole with satisfaction.

Babe gathered a few things to add to his bug-out bag and slipped outside his bedroom window, carefully staying in the shadows as he maneuvered the streets and alleys. He grabbed the first cab to come along.

As the cab pulled up to the Chestnut Street house, the gas lamps to either side of the front door flickered, creating mystical images that appeared and just as quickly morphed into another, like a forest sprite or pixie. Besides the outside lamps, there was a glimmer of light from the lounge, which had been ever-present since his childhood. He didn't hang around but quickly entered the house.

If the assassin were worth a damn, they'd have his phone on a tracker; hence he left it back at his place. While the house had been closed since his grandfather's death, it didn't wreak of staleness. He went from room to room. The pantry had plenty of food, and someone had packed the fridge with perishables, which was curious. He took the stairs two at a time—suddenly, his stomach knotted with the intensity of being back in combat. His senses were on high alert, and if he didn't know better, he felt a presence. He slowly opened bedroom doors as if he expected something or someone to lurch out at him.

A frightened voice came from the last closed bedroom. "I got a gun, and I know how to use it. Now you just back on outta here before I call the po-lice."

Clearing his throat, "Ruthie, it's me, Babe."

She switched on a dim light; he guessed the bedside lamp. She bustled around the room, and while tying the sash of her robe around her waist, she opened the door with a bright smile. "Oh my Goodness, look at you. Everything okay, hon? Come to the kitchen and let me fetch you something to eat. What time is it anyway? You sure you okay?"

Hardly able to get a word in edgewise, he quickly interjected, "I'm fine. Thought I'd stay here for a few days, get out of the Quarter." He followed her into the kitchen.

"Boy, you are a sight for sore eyes. I don't want you to think I'm staying here all the time, no. Just making the house look lived in to keep the no-goods from thinking they can break in. Want a sandwich or something more breakfast-like?" She had a wide ear-to-ear grin as she looked at him.

He didn't want to get her involved in the mess or have to explain his thoughts, but since his grandfather had developed a fondness for the gal, he figured he could relax a little. She busied herself getting plates down from the cabinets, setting everything in front of him with a sweet upturned smile. He didn't care if she took up permanent residence there; it was okay with him. "Eggs would be great, ma'am, but how about I make them for you?"

She shushed him, snickered, and lightly slapped him on the shoulder. "P-shaw, you stay right there." She looked at him closely, "You growing your hair, honey?" Then her eyebrows raised, and a smile lit her face. "You got y'self a woman, don't ya? She wants your hair longer? She must be young. I thought you looked mighty fine with close-cropped hair, but if your lady-friend wants it longer, then best you let it grow; just don't grow all that wild face hair, no matter what she says. Keep your beard trimmed like you do." He quietly sat as she expounded on her preferences with men and their appearances. He nodded with an inward chuckle. He was happy to hear that her son would sometimes stay at the house with her. From her remarks, he gathered the son, Clive Cousins, was about his age and had served in the Army. He didn't remember her being so animated, but it was as though she hadn't had company in a while.

His mind drifted as she spoke. The only conveniences he didn't have were the weight bench and chin-lift bar. He made a mental list of what he needed, and it all boiled down to a gym, but he didn't want his name out there, just in case one computer spoke to another, flagging his name. Some of the monsters were techie-trained, and he had no idea how big the operation was and who the players were. He nodded as she continued on her diatribe. One thing was for sure; the lady was lonely. After eating, he did the dishes, and she tried to muscle him from in front of the sink the whole time. They both had to laugh at the absurdity of her intentions.

Ruthie went on about how he looked like his grandfather other than the coloring, which gave him an idea. "Ruthie, you know anything about coloring hair, like if I wanted to change the color of my hair? You'd know where to get the stuff?" Her eyes became wide as saucers.

"Lean your head down to me. Why you want to go and mess up this beautiful hair of yours?" She put her hand to her lips and gasped, "Hon,

I hope it wasn't because I said you looked like Mr. Rune except for the dark—"

He stood tall and took her hands in his. "No, ma'am, thought I'd go for a change." He grinned with his lop-sided smile. "Think I'll look good?" waggling his eyebrows in jest. Once again, she playfully slapped his arm.

"You too much like Mr. Rune. You got that same quick wit and sharp tongue. Darlin', I'm headed back to bed. You have yourself a good rest." He bid her good rest.

Babe inquired about his grandfather's car, an old Mercedes Sedan. It was in the garage and still purred like a kitten, she answered. Ideas rampaged his mind, and he mentioned that he would be out early; he liked running in the park around five in the morning. He made a mental list of the things he'd need to accomplish—color his hair with a grey wash, step one, and change things up a bit, like a new identity. The ever-present thought was getting his hands on Chop, and he'd get answers, one way or another. If Chop was so terrified of the cartel, even though they were evil incarnate, Babe figured he probably wasn't too far off the same mark and knew he could easily be just as monstrous in the right circumstances. His supposed comrade would learn the hard way, and he knew exactly where to dispose of the body. He'd run that route before with Trinity's ex-brother-in-law, Philip, and his low-life piece-of-shit accomplice.

The plans were to call the Pensacola Beach Holiday Inn Resort and find out if the helicopter tours were still close to their property. If so, he'd grab Chop and bring him to Chestnut Street, remembering to take the battery out of his phone. He'd make him poof, disappear, like a fart in the wind. A warmth ran through his body, relaxing his shoulders, and the weight of anger had melded into contentment. The bullshit would be over soon.

Was the cartel using Chop to do the dirty deeds? Who orchestrated the plot to kill him, and why? Was it just Chop moving the drugs for the cartel? He was pretty sure helo pilots were not that hard to come by. True, he was gutsy, but others might be for the right price. With Chop out of the picture, then Babe would no longer be a person of interest for the cartel. Most of the untidiness was of Chop's making. There was no doubt in his mind that he or someone in his inner circle was the interested buyer for trafficking Trinity, and he hadn't come to Louie's to find him; Chop came to get a handle on her and was probably just as shocked to see Babe as Babe was to see him. *Funny how things go full circle*, he thought. The pieces were dropping right into place.

The wired pilot waited with nervous energy, his knees in constant motor motion, waiting for the phone call. How was he going to explain missing such a big target? Never in a million years did he anticipate seeing Vicarelli in the bar where the girl worked. He wished he'd never gotten the phone call from the punk wannabe about the girl. He couldn't believe she was Cap's woman. Had he known from the beginning, he would never have said yes or relayed some golden opportunity to his drug chief. The whole thing was nothing less than FUBAR—yeah, fucked up beyond all recognition.

While his boss was scary as hell, known for skinning people alive, his military guy was equally frightening. The man could literally pull him apart limb from limb. If Babe ever found out that his supposed friend had been the one trying to traffic his girl, it was going to be horrific. A cold chill ran through his body, causing an involuntary shiver and a cold sweat. He knew it would be lights-out and, in the most horrible way imaginable.

His phone went off. "You take care of things?" The voice on the other side of the phone asked.

"Um, well, I will. The guy bent down just as I took the shot, and then he looked up to the window. I ducked in time that he didn't see, but I'm gonna get him." He could see his hand shaking and knew his voice probably sounded scared shitless.

"I don't give a fuck about the guy; get any decent-looking girl and some more of the kids. No one's looking for them, and they don't compromise me. Your job is to make my life easy, but right now, gringo, you're just a pain in my fucking ass and creating complications in my business. I got more pilots; remember that." Disconnect. He leaned over and vomited outside the car window.

"What'd he say?" Jon, Chop's brother, looked into his twin's face with the same fear that triggered the instantaneous projectile vomit. Jon knew his brother was coloring way beyond the lines and was too deep to rectify the situation. Not only was he dealing dope and abducting innocent people, but by striking deals with the devil, he entered the rings of hell with those he was trafficking.

"I'm fucked, Jon, that's what he implied. He wants more kids and women, nothing to do with the big guy. The thing is, Vicarelli isn't some ordinary jarhead. The man is sharp with a scary extra sense; he sees and knows things other people don't. One fucking scary dude."

Jon drummed his fingers to the beat of the music playing on his radio. "Okay, then, I say, snag a couple of kids; that's what he really wants; the girls are more lagniappe. Pick up one of the hookers on the corner of Canal and Decatur. I'll round up the kids, and you get the girl. Meet you by the Museum in City Park, then get 'em to the copter, and away you go." Jon dropped him off at his car. The plan was in place. "All will be cool. Stop wiggin'."

Chop drove slowly along Decatur, slow enough that it was apparent he was looking for action. He looked in his rearview mirror, popped a breath mint to camouflage the sour remnants of vomit, and then their eyes met. The hot pink chin-length wig combined with her attire, a short shiny black skirt and silver sequined halter top, made her stand out from the other ladies sashaying back and forth. Most of them looked young, but she looked even younger than the rest. Chop guessed maybe fourteen, although she'd probably want men to think she was twenty. He was never good at pickup lines or answers.

Knowing the desperation and distraction caused by angst, he felt sure his voice would sound shaky or go up an octave, making him most undesirable, perhaps sketchy. The street girls were savvy to unhinged lunatics, suspiciously cold degenerates, and regular guys just looking for a quick well-practiced blow job. He took a few deep breaths filling his lungs, hoping to calm his outward appearance and quell his nervous and warry voice.

She walked up to his open passenger window. "Hey, honey, looking for a date?" She winked, suggestively raising her eyebrows.

He smiled and answered, "Yes indeed, beautiful. Get in." He beckoned her in with a flick of his wrist.

"Darlin', I gotta see some green first; a girl can't be too careful." Chop fanned out a few hundred dollar bills so she could see. "Alright, Daddy, you got plenty for a variety of pleasures." She opened the door and slid into the car. "What's ya name, and what kind of game? I'm Candy."

All he could think was, *I bet you are.* He handed the girl a vial of coke. Her eyes lit up, and she took the glass cylinder, stuck her fingernail in, held the scoop under her nostril, and gave it a quick snort. Chop turned onto Canal Street, heading away from the river toward City Park. He lit a joint and took a small, almost negligible hit on it, making sure not to inhale the smoke. She didn't notice and took it, drawing deep not once but three times. Chop thought that would probably do it. The girl began to speak, "Ya neva told me ya name, and how can I pleasure you?"

He looked over at her and smiled. In his head, he started counting down from fifty. "Tim. What's your best talent?" still grinning at her. She reached over and started to unzip his jeans. He held up one finger, continuing to count in his head. She babbled on, and slowly her words began to drift together. "That's some insane weed, wow." He pulled himself out of his pants, grabbed the back of her neck, and lowered her head onto him. She went to work, but he could feel her gradually succumbing to the sedation laced in the weed. He hoped she'd at least be able to finish the job, but no such luck, and she passed out in his lap with her mouth still open around him. "Oh well." He shrugged.

The light changed to red as he pulled up to City Park Boulevard. He waited. There was a lifted truck waiting beside him. The guy driving looked over and chuckled, telling his passenger, who leaned forward and gave Chop a thumbs-up as the two guys cracked up, then the light changed. He passed where the statue used to be displayed. It had been a beautiful work of art and always adorned with seasonal flowers. It had been a landmark used by many. The floral display was there, but no longer the statue, and it wasn't like they had cleaned anything up from the destruction. "Fucking mayor, fucking politics." He turned and headed straight to the New Orleans Museum of Art. He took a right leading him around to the back of the museum, where he pulled behind Jon. He pushed the girl off him and back into her seat, where she puddled like a ragdoll. He got out, zipped up, and went around.

Meanwhile, Jon opened the sliding door on the side where two unconscious boys sprawled. After adding Candy into the van, they bound their hands and feet and tied gags around their heads. Jon dragged the door closed. "Tim, dude, the weed gets 'em every time. Boy, they thought I was cool and never questioned where I was taking them. Job done. So, did your girl complete the exercise?" he chortled. It was a standing joke; they never did. I guess you gotta choke the chicken." He chuckled again. "If it were me, I'd wait to give the girl the joint, but that's me."

Babe looked in the mirror at his weirdly-grey hair, "Fuck me. Not my look, for sure." While it didn't make him look like a much older man, it changed his appearance, especially with the shaggy hair. The color change emphasized the disheveled look. He certainly didn't resemble himself, especially driving a Mercedes Sedan. He needed a good run, a shower, and then to stake out Chop's tour site until he returned, which Babe knew he'd eventually have to do—a waiting game. Babe was proficient in laying wait for prey; some of his missions were a wait to wait, then bam go, go, go, balls to the wall. While Chop was much smaller than him, he was a scrappy fighter and wouldn't be a walk in the park, that is, if he wasn't too stoned, and then if he were loaded, it'd be easy like distracting Gunner with a toss of a ball or squeaky toy. The more he thought about it, the more he imagined Chop was the interested party in Trinity's abduction.

Babe completed his tasks, and it was time for his run in the park. He drove to the front of Audubon and pulled in. Grabbing a bottle of water, the big man donned his grandfather's sunglasses, got out of the car, and began his run. His mind raced with images from past hallucinations wondering why he'd had so few demons stalking him since he began the exploration of his mind. He started picking apart different times in his life, trying to piece together and recreate exercises to sharpen his senses. He focused on the surroundings, listening to every chirp of a bird, zeroing in on where the tweet or song originated. His awareness steadily became more astute as he made his way to Magazine Street, where he crossed over and took a right until the levee was in view.

A couple of kids on electric skateboards approached and swerved out of his path, apologizing all the while. Kid One hollered to Kid Two, "Did you see how ripped that old guy was?" His size and build blew the boys away, and from their comment, he speculated they thought his age to be around fifty—but to kids, anything older than forty was old. *Good*, Babe reflected, not that kids were particularly good at guessing people's ages. He remembered thinking thirty was ancient, and here he was, fastly approaching thirty-seven, a stone's throw from forty. *Fuck, forty*. Trinity was in her twenties. If there were ever to be any children in his future, it was perfect that she was so young.

A warmth spread in his chest as he thought of his grandfather, and then the cramping ache of emptiness from missing him set in. He wished he had confided about the demons, hallucinations, and dreams of killing his father. During one of their meals, he started to mention Trinity but thought an introduction would be better. He would have loved her effervescent personality and, no doubt, appreciated her beauty. She was beautiful, and he missed her. The emptiness spread as he pictured her. He recalled her face in detail. She was similar to her father but had eyes like her mother, almost cat-like, prominent, and slightly swept upward. They were the darkest brown possible, making her pupils indistinguishable. Trinity's skin was like velvet, so soft, and the caramel tone was, to him, exquisite, not too light or dark, in essence, perfect. She was, yes, perfect for him.

The ground on the levee was harder than expected in some places and mucky in others, making for a heads-up run. Upon seeing the massive Ochsner Medical Center in the skyline, he changed direction and headed back for the car. He'd worked up a healthy sweat, and getting back to the house for a shower would be invigorating.

All three victims were out for the count, so Chop drove through McDonald's, taking his time heading back to Pensacola. He had a feeling of accomplishment; the fear of Javier and his wrath had waned. There hadn't been the slightest movement from the back of the van. He no longer had remorse, remembering the first abduction where he cried the whole way to Pensacola; those pitiful feelings were long gone. He'd already appeased his conscience by thinking that if the kids had stayed where they belonged with their parents at home and the hookers had chosen a different line of work, they wouldn't have ended up in the back of his van awaiting a life of slavery.

Before getting on the interstate, he filled his tank and bought a pack of cigarettes. He was now on his time and didn't need to feel the anxiety and apprehension involved in the abduction. He needed the veil of night to transfer the merchandise from the van to the helicopter. It was rare that he'd have a request for an evening experience, maybe sunsetting, but not once the sun had set. He turned on the cruise control and sat back, listening to the radio.

Babe figured Ruthie would be caring for another patient by the time he returned to the house; nonetheless, he scoped his surroundings, checking for anyone following him. His confidence in changing his image had grown, but he didn't want to get over-confident and screw the pooch. He stealthfully entered through the back door, trying to move swiftly but without noise. To his surprise, Ruthie was in the kitchen. "Lawdy, Lawdy, boy, you went and did it. You don't look nothing like yourself. Now don't tell me that lady friend wants you bleached out and grey." She watched him closely, slightly turned her head, raising an eyebrow. "You trying to hide from someone? Is that it?" She put her hand on her hip with intense squinted eyes. "I know you're not in trouble, but is someone after you?" He shook his head, dismissing her question, but she stood blocking him, giving him no choice but to stop. He certainly wasn't going to pick her up. He looked upward and closed his eyes for a moment.

Babe looked down at her. "You don't want to know, ma'am. Have no fear; I have not put you in danger." He started to move around her. But she shuffled to the side blocking him again and shaking her finger at him.

"No, sir. I'm not scared for me, but if you need my help, I got a son, as I told you, not as big as you, but not far off. Now spill the beans."

Babe cracked his one-sided smile. He admired she was one tough bird. "Ruthie, it's all good. Yes, I had a close altercation with a vehicle, and I believe it was intentional, but have no fear; I got this. Right now, I gotta get in the shower and on the road. I plan on confronting the son of a bitch, and he's the one that should be worried. Understand? Now, I am going upstairs, and unless you want to follow me to the bathroom, I think I've said enough to stay your curiosity. How about I'll tell you when I return?" She moved to the side, letting him pass.

"And I want all the details when you get back." *How Trinity of her. Maybe it was women in general.*

A BIRD IN THE HAND

$\mathcal{G}$etting on the interstate was a snap. Driving the sedan was a vast difference from the truck. Before Babe knew it, the speedometer read one ten. "Shit, it doesn't feel that fast." He checked the rearview and side mirrors; luckily, he didn't have a state trooper flying after him. Cruising at eighty miles an hour would be the fastest he'd go. In the truck, he felt every dip and inconsistency on the road emphasizing the miles per hour. Traffic was moving fast, and sometimes it seemed his eighty miles per hour was as though he were standing still. He upped it to eighty-five, remaining slower than some of the yahoos on the road.

He decided to call Trinity since his isolation experiment had gone by the wayside. Yes, he felt he'd overcome and eliminated a few of his demons, but many were left to address. Calling Trinity was playing off the plan, but it felt right.

The phone rang three times and went to her voicemail. "Hi, you've reached Trinity, and if that's not who you're looking for, then you're the one missing out!" *What the hell kind of message was that? Who says that? The one missing out?* The thoughts came to an abrupt halt. He tried to pigeonhole the meaning of his puzzlement, maybe even bordering on anger. Those things had never crossed his mind; in fact, he generally didn't listen to recordings and surely didn't leave messages. Hell, he barely ever called anyone. Tick, tick, tick. Outloud, he blurted, "I'm fucking jealous; what the fuck?" Even though he knew it was stupid, he texted her anyway. It certainly wasn't the intelligent thing to do while traveling at a speed of eighty-five.

Text: *Checking in. Not my phone left it at my place purposefully. Yes, it's me.*

Moments later, the phone buzzed. Babe knew the number; Trinity was calling him after reading the text. As he figured she hadn't answered because of the unknown number.

"Yes?"

"Oh my God, Babe, where the hell are you, and whose phone is this? Are you okay?" Her voice was jittery.

He calmly answered her. "I'm fine. I finished the puzzle, I think. Most of the pieces fit anyway. If all goes as expected, I'll be back in the city late tonight or tomorrow. More processing to navigate." Silence. She started to speak a few times and cut herself off. "What?" he asked, drumming his thumbs on the steering wheel. "What is it? Are you okay?" Now his focus was strictly on her, and he could feel his blood begin to rise. *And that's why calling her was not in the plan—just the opposite!*

"Um, I've been terrified. Don't get angry, but a Marine guy came looking for you. I've heard the name before, Hurley. Anyway, I told him you had gone camping, I thought that made sense, and I had no idea where. Then, I thought I'd call you and let you decide. I've tried to call you for two days, so—" she hesitated.

"So?" he was no longer fearful of her safety or wellness but becoming impatient. She'd done something and was avoiding confession.

"I went by your place." She audibly sucked a breath in, "and when you didn't answer," she raced through the end of her sentence, "I shimmied through your bedroom window." He could picture her raising her shoulders, turning her palms up, squinting her eyes, and putting a sheepish grin on her face.

He nodded, acknowledging his thoughts. The paranoia had been so great that he left through the window; thus, the window was unlocked—his sketchy head. "Things there alright?" He knew how he'd left it; it wasn't clean and organized, which might have panicked her. She knew about his grandfather but had no idea where he had lived or that Babe had sought reclusivity there. "The place looks like a tornado went through; it's a mess, I know."

"Babe, it's more than a mess; it looks like my bedroom. Everything is out of place. You're sure you're okay?" He vaguely remembered throwing objects and shoving furniture as barriers, and yeah, it probably looked worse than her bedroom.

"I'm fine. I gotta go now."

She whimpered, "I love you, Babe Vicarelli."

"And I, you," he responded calmly. "Later, my girl."

As he tapped the red dot, he heard her say, be safe, but the call had ended.

Like a loop, he re-evaluated the conversation and forced their Q and A through his mind. He knew he sometimes overthought things, making them much more significant than they were, and perhaps this was such the case. Babe knew he loved her, but, as he'd asked Trey, how to keep it together concerning her safety. He couldn't protect her twenty-four-seven. And what if he had one of the hallucinations and hurt her, thinking she was the enemy? Questions that had no answers, but trust God. *Hm.*

Within the hour, he pulled up to the helicopter tour sign, thought about it, and reversed enough that he had a clear view but wouldn't draw attention. Chop wouldn't be looking for him anyway. He turned the engine off and surfed the web. *Camping?* The last thing he wanted was to sleep under the stars or on the ground. Maybe after a few years, he'd feel differently. There was a peace that only nature provided. And just like that, the God thing came up again. He searched for a Bible app, not one of the ones with thee and thou. He'd sat through religion classes in school and made good grades, but that was the extent of him and religion. He was pretty sure that was as far as it would go. His opinion of the God entity was fairly cemented in his heart. No one could answer where God had been during Trinity's experience.

The thing no one knew at school was the hell he lived with at home. Even though his maimed father could no longer hurt him or his mother physically, his emotional and mental abuse was as bad if not worse than the beating had been.

Headlights approached, passed him without the slightest touch of the brakes, and pulled up, sidling next to the helicopter. Chop was about to unload his cargo—probably stacked and wrapped bundles of cash. Babe got out of the car in silence, skirting the road. The van blocked Chop's sightline enough that Babe could make his way undetected. There was nothing that could have prepared him for the cargo. He moved behind the van and suddenly appeared; the shock was almost jaw-dropping. With a glare, his head barely moving from side to side, he knew, from the horrified expression on Chop's face, that his fuming anger had registered. With determined strides, he approached as the pilot was transferring a woman from the van to the bird.

At first, he could see the confusion on the pilot's face and then the spark of recognition. "Stay out of this, Vic. You don't wanna mess with my boss. You think you're a badass motherfucker; you ain't seen nothing compared to Javier. Now leave me the fuck alone and let me do my job." There was a shakiness in Chop's voice, his apprehension intense. "I mean it, back the fuck off; this ain't your concern. You won't be able to save them all."

"It is my concern, you sick bastard." Babe landed a fist to Chop's throat in a swift, unstoppable strike, making him drop the girl. He caught the girl a split-second before she hit the ground, so it was a softer landing; he looked to his left and saw the boys, one from the group of street kids he'd seen a week or two back. Babe tipped his head to the side, rolling it to the other side with a primal intensity in his eyes. There was no point in killing him right then; he wanted to hear him say he'd been part of Trinity's nightmare. He grabbed the tape from the van they had used on their victims and bound Chop's hands; then, he felt the cold barrel of a gun behind his ear. "Think twice," Babe warned the person with the weapon.

"Fuck you." He heard a click from the gun, and in a fluid motion, he'd redirected the person's arm, and the weapon fired bullets into the air. With the other hand, he shoved the man until he fell onto his back and tried to scramble away. Babe didn't give a shit about the man with the gun and put his boot on the man's throat, pushing hard enough that he could hear a grisly crunch. Chop struggled to get to his feet; the big man kicked him in the gut, bulldozing him backward. He heard a small moan come from the van and saw one of the boys starting to squirm.

Sirens penetrated the night air. With lights flashing and sirens blaring, two police vehicles screeched to a halt. The officers yelled, "Hands where I can see them." Babe raised his arms with his hands extended. He stood statue-still and waited for the officers to approach, knowing they would be quick to subdue and contain him. If it were him, he'd advise the same thing. Babe stayed silent, giving the officers a moment to deduce the situation. With firearms drawn, they approached. "Don't move motherfucker," an officer yelled at him as they tried to lock down the scene. Babe watched their eyes. One lasered on him, and the other was taking account of the bodies. They saw two men unconscious on the ground, one with their hands bound, and a collapsed woman behind the massive man's feet. The drug was wearing off both boys as they struggled against their restraints. Given that Babe hadn't flinched and remained calm, the other officer holstered his gun, cuffed him, and put him in the back of his unit.

By this time, the younger officer had removed the gag and ropes from one boy. "Officer, officer, he's the good guy!" He shouted, pointing toward the police car where Babe was. "That big guy, dude, he was saving us. Those are the douchebags that drugged us." The boy was near hysteria.

"He's not the perve. They are." He frantically waved his hand, pointing to the two men flat on the ground.

The woman began to stir, moving the sand beneath her. Groggily, she asked, "Where the hell am I?" She sat up, blinking hard to clear the fuzz in her eyes, hoping to figure out what happened, then saw Chop on the ground. She screamed and tried to get up but was still too out of it to stand and sat crying and screaming at the abductor. "You fucking asshole. Officer, help! Help me!" she sobbed to the one policeman who was untying the second boy.

He had radioed for the ambulance and backup. There was too much going on for the two of them to secure the scene. Their radios continued to crackle with staticky communication. It had developed into a setting made for the movies—lights continually flashing, radios squawking back and forth. Both boys were now begging for Babe. Ten minutes passed, and none of the officers responded to the woman or boys about the degenerates on the ground. Babe understood; he would've handled it the same way. He knew he was big, and if he'd wanted to create havoc, it would've been hellacious, but he didn't. He wanted the police to take the brothers; eventually, they'd understand the situation. Babe would roll with the flow and be the model of civility and calm; these were rough seas at best. His gut said Chop's brother was dead; he hoped not, given the new situation; they'd charge him with murder.

With the scene under control, paramedics had triaged and were tending to Chop's brother, who was hanging on by a thread. Babe figured he'd be dead on arrival and was somewhat surprised that he was still alive. The three victims and two men left with the paramedics in ambulances, and the police hauled Babe to the police station.

While riding in the car, he remained silent, waiting for someone to ask him something. They led him to a holding cell. He patiently waited, imagining they'd send someone to interrogate him, but he had an inkling of how it would go. He was a threat in the eyes of the officers, no ands or buts, even though he hadn't said or done anything to confirm their suspicions. The mere fact of his size often put him in the wrongdoer category.

Sitting alone in the cell, he had nothing to do but sit and think of similar situations. No matter the situation as a kid in school, he was always the one escorted to the principal's office only to be returned to class, the play yard, or the cafeteria once an adult took the time to find out what happened. Still, they always assumed he was at fault from the beginning. Bigger wasn't always better.

For some reason, boys and men wanted to fight him, yet he didn't engage; he usually held them off and waited for an authority figure to appear. Only once in high school had he felt pushed too far, but even then, all he did was subdue the instigators. That's the first time he met Jack Kennedy, the wrestling coach. Jack watched as two boys antagonized the hell out of Babe and waited to see how the oversized lad would handle it. It wasn't until one of the boys became physical that the big boy responded and put one of the kids on the floor while getting a headlock on the other. That was the day Coach Kennedy entered Babe's life, and the two kids were sent to the office, not him, for a change.

The sound of approaching footsteps echoed off the walls as the officer that brought him to the station arrived at the doorway with another man, he figured a detective. The young-looking policeman spoke, "I told you the guy was big, but Sarge, he's been completely cooperative. The two kids, tied up in the back of the van at the scene, screamed for this guy. According to them, he was saving them." He pointed his chin at Babe.

The guy in civies stood by the cell, taking a long look at him. He unlocked the cell and opened the door. The three men sat at a table in the room. "From your license, I see your name is Babe R. Vicarelli. Is that correct?" Babe nodded. "Mr. Vicarelli, have you been read your rights?"

"Yes, sir, and I waved them." Babe gave a quick upturn of his lips.

The man continued, "Can you explain to me, Mr. Vicarelli, the activity tonight at the beach?"

Babe, while a big guy, was somewhat soft-spoken with a clear definitive voice when he chose to be. "Yes, sir. The helicopter pilot served in the military with me and had recently contacted me in New Orleans, where I live. After only a scant amount of time, it was apparent he was not the person I remembered from Afghanistan. He gave me a sob story about his wife, who had gone missing. He asked for my help; he said he'd tried to report it to y'all, which I wasn't sure was true, but I drove to Pensacola to try to help. After checking things out, I suspected he was running drugs, I asked, and he confirmed it with me. I told him to get his life together and that I wanted nothing to do with him." He stopped speaking for a moment letting his words get absorbed and deciding how much he wanted to disclose while sizing up the two men in front of him. "Even though it was not my place, I felt like I needed to try to help him onto the right road one more time, and then I'd be done if he walked away or refused. He was a helluva helo pilot and saved my ass several times in combat. I felt I needed to do him a solid." Both the men nodded in understanding.

Babe tucked his lips over his teeth, sucked in, and let out a deep sigh. "I watched as he pulled the van up to the bird. I was going to confront him, and that's when I saw he had an unconscious woman in his arms, transferring her from the van to the helo; I had to stop him. I relieved him of the lady and put him on the ground securing his hands. He also had two semi-conscious teenage boys tied up in the back of his vehicle. I recognized one of the kids from New Orleans. He's a street kid; I've given him a few bucks for food, but that's beside the point. While I restrained Tim Faraday, his brother came from behind and put a gun to my head. I disarmed him and, in the process, rendered him unconscious. I heard when the weapon engaged, and I acted on reflex. The gun went off as I struck his arm, and it wasn't much longer when the units pulled to the scene. I thought he was moving drugs, not women and kids, and those are the facts, gentlemen."

The detective scribbled some words on a piece of paper inside a file on the desk. "Mr. Vicarelli, I'm going to put you back in holding until I corroborate your story." The three got up, and he returned Babe to the cell. "Yaeger is going to stay here, and as soon as we've ascertained that your accounting is accurate, I'll give him the go-ahead, and you'll be released. If not, it'll be a whole different conversation, and you'll be with us to process." Babe nodded. He knew his accounting would hold up, and he'd be out of there. How long it would take would be anyone's guess.

As the detective started out of the room, Babe asked for his phone. Not that he had anyone he planned on calling, but at least he could surf; after all, it wasn't his phone, but his grandfather's. The detective nodded to the uniform, and the two left the room. Once again, he heard their footsteps as they faded down the hall. Patrolman Yaeger quickly returned, asking if he could get Babe some water.

"No, but thanks."

The officer sat at the table, and he could see the young man was nervous as he nibbled his fingernails while his knees hyper-bounced, and he pensively scanned the room like Gunner did when they opened the can of dog food, waiting for them to scoop it into the bowl. "Uh, Mr. Vicar—"

"Babe," he corrected with a slight one-sided grin. There was always a reaction. Not that he cared, but Steve, Bill, or Tom would've been so much easier. There was the added consequence of his name that could be good or bad; most people wouldn't forget it.

"How long were you in the military, and what branch?" With a nervous rambling of thoughts and an occasional stutter, the officer continued babbling, not giving Babe an opportunity to respond, which was fine. He was probably mid-twenties at the most, had a shiny gold band on his left hand, maybe a newlywed, and a baby face, which may have made him look younger than he actually was. Then he sat and awkwardly smiled; Babe waited to see if he had finished speaking. He had.

"Eleven plus years. Marine Corps. How long have—"

Cutting the big man off, "A year," he responded enthusiastically. "Mostly, we get calls about kids having too much to drink or being rowdy." *Kids?* *You're a fucking kid,* went through Babe's mind. The officer chattered about life as a policeman in Pensacola Beach for the next half hour. He emphasized there was more activity than people might think; it wasn't all bikinis and hot chicks. Babe nodded, glancing between him and the phone as he searched for articles or information about Mays Connolly, his older brother that he may one day meet, but maybe not. Everything he read re-hashed the same things he'd already seen, nothing new. The man was, from all he'd read, a standup guy. Thoughts rambled through his mind keeping time with the incessant hour-long jabber of Officer Yaeger. Then, the guy's phone rang. "Yes, sir. No, sir. Will do. Oh, Jeez. Yes, sir. Ten-four." He smiled at Babe. "Looks like your story checks out. Oh, and the guy on death's doorstep did pass, but it was from drugs, not any physical injuries. You can go after I finish the paperwork." The deputy left the room. After about a half hour, he returned with a bag containing Babe's personal property, unlocked the cell, and added his last bit of worldly thoughts as he got a signature for the returned items. "Maybe next time, leave catching the criminals to us. Shit, man, you missed getting killed by a hair. It was your lucky night that you were able to knock the gun away. It came close to being your last night on this earth." *Ten-four, wise one.* He chuckled to himself.

As Babe walked out of the cell, he looked down at the younger man and commented, managing to keep a straight face, "I'll take it under advisement." He'd watched as they had driven to the station, figuring it might be a half-hour walk to his car. He wondered *why going to the police station was a one-way ticket, never a return trip.*

After getting to his car, the first stop would be the hospital to check on the kids. He was reasonably confident authorities would contact the parents or a family friend, aunt, uncle, or someone that gave a shit about them. Not that he knew much about kids, but he figured they were probably fifteen or sixteen, but maybe younger.

The traffic was seasonably light, considering it was the time of year for end-of-summer family beach vacations and the last hoorahs of Labor Day festivities around the corner. The heat was bearable with the cool breeze from the Gulf. Babe remembered the hospital from the debacle with Chop's wife; hopefully, it was where they brought the victims. The whole situation with Tim Faraday was enough to boggle the mind. Still, looking back at the acts of courage in Afghanistan, it wasn't balls of steel; he was nuts and liked living on the edge. He was like an adrenalin junkie, and perhaps that was part of it, but now knowing about the addiction aspect, it was more than likely drug-induced bravery.

He pulled into the parking lot near the entrance to the Emergency Room. The waiting area, hardly maxed out, was busier than he had anticipated—two people were ahead of him at a sliding window. The thought jetted through his mind; he didn't know the kids' names or the woman with the pink wig.

It was his turn at the window, and he imagined it was to get his name on a waiting list. A man, probably near his age, was at the window. He had a warm, friendly smile. "How can I help you?"

Babe began to speak, "I don't know the name of the kids or the woman with them, but they were—"

"Your name, sir?" He politely interrupted.

Fishing his license from his pocket, he answered, "Babe Vicarelli. I need to know if the paramedics brought two boys and a woman here or—" He handed the man the license, which it didn't appear as if he cared.

The nurse put his hand up. "I am glad to see you. The two boys have been waiting for you and raising quite a stink. From what I understand, it's been a colorful night." He smiled and pointed to his right. "When the door clicks, you'll be able to push it open and retrieve the two teens." Babe acknowledged and thanked the man.

Once through the door, he felt like he'd entered utter chaos, with the intensity almost of a war zone. He guessed, in a way, it was; much of the activity might have been life or death. Even though it felt like pandemonium, there was an element of fluidity between the doctors, nurses, techs, and personnel. A few hustling people stopped turning toward Babe and smiled. He guessed the boys must've been making a ruckus, and everyone was glad he had arrived.

A cute young blonde-haired nurse smiled with the same perfect set of symmetrical dimples as Jessica Lambert, the girl that had died during Spring Break in New Orleans. He reminisced, thinking she was probably the same age, twenty-one or so. "Right this way, sir. The doctor has checked the boys thoroughly, and the discharge papers are ready for you to sign. I'll send the doctor in if you need to talk to him, but all the information is in the paperwork, and I'll review it with you. I imagine it's been a stressful night, but worry not; they've been in good hands." Babe nodded and thanked her as they pulled the curtain aside and turned into the cubicle. "They insisted on staying together and cut up when we tried to separate them." She sweetly smiled.

Both boys sat on the bed and jumped up as he and the nurse entered. "What's with the new hair, dude?" One of the boys asked, but they both had their heads cocked in curiosity. "I knew you'd come. See, Reg; I told you he'd find us." The slightly smaller boy chucked the other's shoulder as he spoke.

The nurse took a few papers out of the chart. "When you get them home, all they need is a good shower and clean clothes. Poor things, they must have been terrified until they saw you and then to have you taken away—" She shook her head back and forth with empathy. To the boys, she smiled, "Well, he's here now, right?" Then she looked at Babe and handed him a form to sign for their discharge. She led them from the emergency room with a tight-lipped smile and glossy eyes as though on the verge of tears. "Enjoy the ride home, and sir, they didn't cut up too bad; they're boys, after all."

Babe turned to face her, "There was a lady with a pink wig, as well. Is she here?" Crinkling her brow and somewhat confused, she nodded. "I asked because I have room in my car if she needed a ride back to New Orleans. It's better than someone having to pick her up or getting a bus ticket home. Just sayin'." He shrugged a shoulder.

"I'll ask, but I'm not so sure she'd want to get in the car with a stranger; I mean—" She raised her eyebrows. "You seem like a nice man, and the boys think the world of you, but you know what I mean. I'll give it a whirl. Wait here, and I'll let you know in a minute." The three sat in the waiting room. If he were any judge of character, which he felt he was, he'd lay odds that Miss Pink Wig was a working girl and getting in a stranger's car was commonplace. Given the recent circumstances, she may be leery, but it was worth the offer. He didn't have ulterior motives; he was just trying to be a good guy. *Here's to you, Trey,* he thought.

The clickety tap of spike heels against the floor echoed from the other side of the door. A nasally-sounding voice spoke as the door opened. "Thanks, girl." She smiled at the nurse, turned on her heel, and approached the man and two boys, giving him a thorough assessment. "Whoa, you're a big guy. I'm Candy, and you are?" She flashed a flirty smile and a bat of eyelashes.

"Babe Vicarelli. I thought you might need a ride back to the city, nothing more." She understood his meaning. He wasn't looking for her services. "Ma'am, you've had yourself a helluva night, I'd say. Shit, it's damn near daybreak. This way to the car."

THE ANSWER, NO ANSWER

*B*road washes of color crested along the horizon, announcing another day, a reminder that he hadn't conquered his demons, and he came to the realization they'd probably never go away. Perhaps, he hoped, they would continue to lessen with time, and maybe they already had a little bit. His heart felt assured that it was Tim Faraday attempting to assassinate him—the why of it all would remain a mystery for the time being. By now, the police undoubtedly had a handle on the accurate picture and had him on multiple charges; all were severe enough to put him away for many years. *Threat eliminated.* The question ticking through his mind was to return to isolation or take one day at a time, hoping Trinity would understand the ride and not bail. He still knew he had to toughen mentally and sharpen his awareness.

The morning traffic was a beast, and as they rode through New Orleans East, he flashed back to Trinity's harrowing experience. For a moment, he felt at peace, knowing he'd added two more bodies to the plethora of burned-out vehicles occupied by the dead—some warranted such an ending, and others were victims of heinous crimes, deserving so much better. Those poor souls would be at the banquet with God if Heaven truly existed. Unfortunately, he'd witnessed and survived enough to give him a slant of unbelief, but for Trinity, he'd try. If Trey were correct, saying God was legit, and it would lessen his worry, then that would be a bonus, but he still looked at it like some child's bedtime story.

Sounds of sleeping purrs from the kids created a peaceful lull in the car. Candy was far more restless than the boys. In her profession, picking up lunatic johns had to be an ever-present concern. He knew the stories behind some of the call girls, which ranged from paying their way through college to earning enough to support a child or a drug habit. He passed no judgment; people did what they had to for survival. Not that he needed or wanted to know why the girl chose the life she did. He'd spent enough time thinking about his passenger and turned his mind to his spitfire girlfriend.

Warmth passed through his body in rolling waves, creating a tickle of sorts, and it seemed to stir in his body whenever his mind drifted to his lady. She was the one constantly questioning him, and maybe because he wasn't what one would call a lady's man or people person, he hadn't pried into hers. Perhaps he needed to engage and learn about her childhood, upbringing, and how she ended up content at Louie's. The beat of his heart sped up, pounding faster and harder thinking of her, but it also illuminated the frustration with the roll-and-go traffic on the high-rise bridge into the city.

Miss Pink Wig righted herself, stretching and yawning with all the daintiness of the mules that pulled the carriages through the quarter. She pulled down the visor, flicked open the lighted mirror, and with a slight gasp, adjusted her wig, which had slid off-center. Licking her fingertip, she wiped remnants of smeared makeup from under her eyes and looked at Babe. "Ya coulda told me I looked like shit," she raised an eyebrow and cocked her head to the side. "Do I know you? I don't forget faces, and I think I do. You were with that tiny Hispanic girl. Yeah," she nodded her head. "Tiny little thing."

"She's not Hispanic, not that it makes a difference. She's Creole, a combination of French and Haitian or African, I think. She tends bar at Louie's Tap." He continued looking straight ahead, hoping for a break in the traffic. It seemed he was in the only lane not moving.

98

"Oh. I thought, never mind." *She better not say they were in the same line of work, or her ass will be walking the rest of the way.* He could feel his body stiffen with anger. It was better to stop the conversation. "Can you drop me by my place on Canal Street?" His bottom jaw jutted forward as his teeth gnashed together, but he nodded with a half smile.

Babe wanted to get home to Trinity in the worst kind of way. *What about the boys?* He didn't want to drop them at Jackson Square. He didn't have room in his place for anyone to live with him, but he did at Chestnut Street. His mind began to churn the possibilities. He'd inherited more money than he could spend in a lifetime, especially given his frugal lifestyle. A thought crossed his mind: Ruthie might take a shine to the boys, but they'd have to go to school. There were no freeloaders in his world. Houseguests were more of a check-with-Trinity-kind of thing, so he stabled the idea until he could talk with her.

Chris, the older dirty brown-haired boy, spoke, "Dude, I never figured you for a Mercedes kinda person. You seem more like a Jeep or a truck or maybe a Harley, but Mercedes, this is a pawpaw car, and you ain't no pawpaw, but what's with the grey hair and scruffy beard? Man, you don't look like you." Babe glanced in the rearview, and he sure as hell didn't look like himself. In a deep rumble, he chuckled. The boy quickly said, "I mean, no offense, dude. Thanks for picking us up and for the lift to the city."

In that smattering of a few moments, he decided to drop the hooker at her place and then drop the boys at his place for a shower with strict instructions not to touch a thing in his apartment, but then he remembered how torn up he'd left it, according to Trinity. He'd drop Miss Pink Wig and pick up Trinity. It'd be her first visit to Chestnut Street.

He called her, knowing she was probably sleeping as it was only eight-thirty. She answered in a hoarse, groggy voice, "You okay?"

"Morning, and yes, I'm fine" He was quick to answer. "Can you be ready in about a half-hour? I'll pick you up in front of the hotel if you want. I'm in a black sedan."

Her voice sounded more awake in a matter of seconds, and he could hear her moving into high gear. "I'll be waiting outside. I can't wait to see you."

Seeing her reaction to the grey hair and unkempt beard would be interesting. He'd never been one for beards until his last deployment, and he remembered his face itched like tiny gnats were constantly biting. That was how it felt at that moment, nasty, dirty, and scraggly. Scratching his face while immediately feeling better only ramped up the itching sensation to an unbearable degree, kinda like the sand fleas of Afghanistan. Those horrid insects carried disease and laid their eggs in open wounds. They were vile creatures of mammoth annoyance. The shit on his face was hours away from a good clean-up. He knew she liked the close-cropped well-manicured beard, and this wild unkempt look was not his jam.

It wasn't long before they pulled up to the girl's apartment. "Thanks, hon." She went to kiss him on the cheek, but he pulled back, with the thought of, who knew where those lips had been. *Thank you, no!* His body had an inward shiver of disgust. He wasn't judging but, nonetheless, wasn't interested in the gesture. She exited the car and climbed the steps to her apartment, which was a house turned fourplex, maybe even more. He watched as she dug in a plant beside the door producing a key, unlocked the door, and with a slight wave, he pulled away.

He made a beeline to Hotel Noelle. Trinity was standing outside in a colorful billowy top, cutoff jeans, strappy sandals, and black sunglasses that took up half her face. Like waving bon voyage on the side of an ocean liner, she exuberantly hailed him, pointing at the car as if to say, who's car?

He pulled to the curb and got out, meeting her halfway in front of the car. Bubbles burst inside his gut, something akin to butterflies but bigger and far more fluttery. She wrinkled her forehead. "Wow, new color, different facial hair, and boy, your hair has grown, and it's only been a week." She reached up and pulled his head down to her, grabbing a handful of hair. "Give us some sugar; I've missed you." He held her tightly, saying there was much to talk about. The melding of her body next to his radiated a heat wave starting from the tips of his ears and all the way down. "I can tell you missed me too. It feels like ages, and I want you, Babe Vicarelli, in a most naughty way." He opened her door, and she slid in. "I guess the car is part of the 'much to talk about' you mentioned." He nodded with a full-lopsided smile. As she settled in the car, she turned to face the two boys in the back seat. "And so are those?" speaking of the kids.

The older boy introduced himself as Chris and the other as Reg. Both boys were hyper with chatter, trying to tell her about their ordeal, but between the two, it was hard to make sense of their chopped-up story. Just from the bit she gleaned, Babe was correct; there was much he needed to tell her. While it was only a week and a day, it had been a long week for her Marine. She saw the wear on his face, and it hurt her heart.

Babe slid behind the wheel, and off they headed for St. Charles Avenue. Every other second he glanced her way. She was beautiful and his, and nothing was going to come between them again. Trinity touched on the few strangers who came to the bar looking for him, which they'd discuss later. *Hm. Interesting*, he thought.

Babe swung into the driveway and parked. They entered through the side door, nobody saying a word, yet an emotional chasm of silence was deafening. Trinity looked at Babe, turning her hands up as if to say, where are we? He wasn't quite sure how to respond; the answer still tugged on his heart, developing a lump in his throat. Yes, it was his house, but no, it was his grandfather's. He'd seen many men die, but the death of Rune hadn't settled, and he didn't know if it ever would. He'd often said selling the house was the only option, yet he hadn't taken that step, so was it the only option?

He spoke to Trinity within earshot of the boys answering unasked questions; now everybody would understand. "This was my grandfather's home, and now the house belongs to me." The statement came with a momentary half-hearted smile. The ache lingered in his soul.

"It's spectacular, Babe. Why don't you move here?" She was exuberant, like finding the prize at the bottom of the cereal box.

His eyes told the story with a longing to live closer to her and to what was comfortable. The big house wasn't his style, at least not yet, and he questioned if it would ever be comfortable without his grandfather. At the same time, it was worth nearly two million dollars plus furnished with the finest antiques, and maybe one day, it'd feel right. For now, living a bare-to-the-bone existence felt more like his lifestyle.

The question lingered, what was Trinity used to? Her apartment was upscale, and the Lakeview house was in the upper end of middle class or lower end of the upper class. While she had dug deep with persistent questions to learn about the big guy, knocking down the emotional barricades, he knew very little about her other than in the moment. Counting the things he knew, he began a mental list. She came from a large family, one of seven children; she had a house in Lakeview and an apartment through the hotel. He'd understood that her father, while dressed in five thousand dollar suits, had business practices that stepped across the border of propriety and pushed the rules—nothing as despicable as the cartels with their human and major drug trafficking.

Antoine Noelle lined the pockets of city officials to overlook any construction allowances, bending the rules to suit his needs. He, while not said, merely inferred that he eliminated any blocks to his plans. Mr. Noelle was a local law bender and one of those people who came across like he was above the law. Her mother seemed kind and proper, but wasn't it the usual situation for many men who danced with crime?

Babe watched Trinity walk from room to room, followed by the two boys. He told the boys to take showers upstairs; they needed one. He continued, "Toss your clothes over the railing, and I'll get them in the wash. There's soap and shampoo already in the showers. Wrap a towel around yourself and lounge in a bedroom, but not the one occupied by Ruthie. You'll be able to tell which room is hers."

He could hear the boys checking out the bedrooms and then bickering over who went in what room. Minutes later, the dirty clothes dropped from the banister. Babe picked up the smelly jeans and tee shirts and called Ruthie, asking her to pick up some clothes and the sizes using the household credit card. When she asked how many she'd be cooking for, he answered five, including herself. Trinity intently listened with a frown growing on her face.

When Babe hung up, she turned to him with a look of curiosity. "Vic, what is all this? You've got some explaining to do. Who is Ruthie, and how long has she lived in your house? I mean, what is your relationship with her?" He saw the anger mount as she questioned him. He had a chuckle going on inside. Trinity, always so carefree about anyone talking to him, had extreme feelings about a woman she knew nothing about. An internal debate began deciding if he should let her stew or cut to the chase before she said something she couldn't take back, and he couldn't 'unhear.' He moved toward her attempting to put his arms around her. "Oh, I don't think so. Start explaining, Babe." He coughed out a laugh. "Not funny; I mean it. Is that where you've been or who you've been with?" Should he add fuel to the fire and say only one night or extinguish the flames?

"Trinity, calm down" He stood calmly before her, gazing into her eyes. "Ruthie is the lady that took care of my grandfather. She's in her sixties, I guess. She's a good lady, and I've let her stay here. If that's a problem, I'll tell her to leave. I don't want to leave the house empty, which means I'll have to move here, and I don't want to; I like my place close to you." With a sheepish grin, she said she thought it was a well-thought-out plan to have the woman live at the house. Her eyes were a dead giveaway to her embarrassment over the needless jealousy.

Babe heard the television from upstairs and decided to take a peek. Stealthfully he climbed the stairs and moved just as silently, following the sound. The door was ajar; he glanced into the room and saw both boys sprawled in the bed, towels around their waists, and sleeping soundly. He returned downstairs and reclined on the sofa. She snuggled next to him, and they both drifted to sleep.

They woke to the sound of rustling bags and a creaky door. Ruthie tip-toed into the living room. Babe put his hand in the air, which startled Trinity, causing her to sit upright. The older woman smiled from ear to ear. "You must be the girlfriend. I'm Ruthie; I took care of Mr. Rune before he passed. You are?" She checked Trinity out from head to toe, sizing the young woman up, which gave Trinity the feeling that she needed to stand.

After introducing herself and answering the usual question about her family being those Noelles from the French Quarter, everyone seemed satisfied. Ruthie laid out the clothes she purchased and the receipt for Babe. He hadn't talked to Trinity about the boys, the house, or the events since he last saw her; thus, he switched gears to laundry matters and the clothes in the washer.

Trinity was due at Louie's at four-thirty; therefore, dinner needed to be done by three to make it back for her to change and get to work. After such a tenuous few days, she wanted more quality time with Babe. There was much to discuss. She sent a brief text to Shep.

Trinity: *Do you care if I get Samantha to work for me tonight?*

Shep: *You okay, girl? Sam can work for you. If not, Finn can handle the bar.*

Trinity: *Perf. Let Finn, no Sam.*

Shep: *Works for me.*

Her eyes widened as though alarmed. "Got work sorted; Finn's gonna work the bar," she sighed in relief, but then her eyebrows shot up. "Crap, Vic, we need to get Gunner. I almost forgot. This isn't gonna work; you better drop me at my place, and I'll take Gunn to work with me like usual."

"Leave it to the kid," he casually answered. "Too much to catch up on, right?" He threw one of his spicy looks her way. She giggled at his flirtatious overture. He walked into the kitchen, where Ruthie was chopping the seasoning, prepping for dinner. "There are two boys upstairs napping. They shouldn't be a bother, but if they are, text me. You know how to text? We have to run out for a minute."

She put her hand on her hip and waved a finger at him. "For that, I should slap you upside your head, boy. Do I know how to text; I'm older than you, but not ancient. I even taught your grandaddy to text." She mumbled under her breath, "Do I know how to text?" She shook her head at him and tsked. Ruthie had taken charge, which meant he could sit back and do his thing—tend to Trinity. They headed out the door.

While driving to get Gunner, Trinity started with the questions. "Is this your grandfather's car, and what's the deal with the house? Does Ruthie come with it?" She laughed. Babe explained the details about the house, the car, and the abundance of money left to him. "So, I got a rich and handsome lover. Seems like I struck the Lotto!" They snaked through the Quarter and pulled into the Hotel Noelle parking garage, asking the attendant to keep the car handy as they would only be a half-hour tops.

Trinity was chatty as though starved for Babe's company. Walking up to her front door, they heard the ferocious growling of Gunner. "Hurry before he scratches your door," Babe advised. His four-legged friend jumped all over him as he entered. "I missed you, too, buddy, but calm down." Looking at Trinity, he questioned, "You have spoiled him rotten. Where is my well-behaved canine? This looks like my friend, but he's out of control!" He crouched down to the dog's level. "Gunn," he put his strong and massive hands on the dog's back, encouraging him to sit, which he did. "He'll be back in form within the next few hours, or we'll have a come to Jesus."

Trinity seized the opportunity and said since they were speaking of Jesus, Babe cut her off. He wasn't ready for some deep conversation. He approached with a hungry look in his eye and scooped her up, carrying her to the bedroom. He kissed her hard and deep, nipping at her lips. She turned her head toward him with a euphoric smile. He glanced into her eyes, responding with a quick grin, and they closed her bedroom door.

Their interlude, while fulfilling, was brief. Trinity's voice became timid, "I don't want to be the one to point this out, but you didn't wrap up your pleasure wand. Probably nothing to concern ourselves with, right?" She stayed silent for a moment, then proceeded in a demanding tone. "We gotta do something with that hair, Babe. I know I said I liked it longer, but it's a mess. We have clippers at my parents. My mom used to style Charles and Louis' hair; they got that tightly coarse hair, like her side of the family, whereas Neville, Antoine, and Chance have hair like my daddy, Bethany, and me." She pulled him to a sitting position, climbed on his lap, and put her hands in his hair. She separated the top of his hair and grabbed a hair claw from the side of the bed, clipping the handful. We'll leave this longer but shave this crud," with the other hand, she tugged on the underneath section, and we'll keep the scruff or razor it; I don't care. No bushy beard; it doesn't suit your face, at least this way. It has to be neat to go with you."

He pulled the claw from his hair. "I got an idea shave the whole motherfucker." She screeched in horror and shook her head in defiance with pursed lips and squinted eyes. Babe put his hands up in surrender. "Hey, whatever you want, I really don't care. It's hair, and however you want it is fine with me, but no long man bun, okay?"

Trinity's lips formed the perfect pout asking if she'd upset him. He laughed, dragging her to the shower. They'd spent far more than half an hour; thus, Babe directed a quick shower, swift dressing, and out the door with Gunner. The dog kept to Babe's side going through the hotel, regardless of the leash. It was like a light switched on, and he remembered to follow commands. When they arrived at the parking garage, the attendants had kept his car parked close to the exit. After a brief jaunt and a few turns, they pulled up to Babe's truck. "You want to drive the truck or car?" he asked, knowing she'd probably vote for the car.

As suspected, she chose the car and put Gunner in the back seat. She waited for Babe to pull out and followed close behind. St. Charles Avenue, with its canopy of oak trees, always seemed magical; huge stretched-out branches created picture postcard splendor. The jingling of a street car helped to set the scene. Thoughts scrambled around about the boys and what her man's plans might be. She changed the radio station to energetic, upbeat music, like they played at Louie's, figuring he would come to a decision or ask her opinion. What was her view, if asked? They were street kids, runaways, probably with a myriad of mental, if not behavioral, issues.

Babe took a left on Sixth and then turned on Chestnut a couple of blocks after they passed Prytania. He signaled Trinity to pull into the driveway and closed in behind her. Leaning into the car on the driver's side, he stole a kiss from her while pressing the remote to open the garage. "Can you pull in, or do you want me to?" She slid the car into drive and pulled into the garage. She closed the garage, then she and Gunner came out a side door.

"Can I pull it in, boy, please!" He had to chuckle; she acted indignant, all in play. He leashed Gunner, not knowing how Ruthie would respond to the dog. He unlocked the back door, and the three entered the house. Babe could hear Ruthie and the boys talking. He put a finger to his lips, and they stood quiet for a moment. She was laying down the house rules, friendly, almost motherly, but in a no-nonsense tone. The conversation answered some of Trinity's questions. Whether Babe had planned on taking the boys in or not, Ruthie had decided for him.

"How're things going?" He, Trinity, and Gunner entered the dining room. She had prepared a feast for the boys and had them dressed in their new togs. An old black chalkboard was on the table. Babe chuckled to himself, finding it amusing.

"Lordy, Lordy, you bringing an animal into your grandfather's home? Is he house-trained and well-behaved? He won't be jumping up on the furniture, and what about doing his business? I don't know about a dog on these pine floors. What would Mr. Rune say?" Dramatic changes were happening fast. He could imagine him and Trinity staying there on Sundays, but not every day for sure.

He picked up the chalkboard and grinned. "Ruthie, you sure you weren't in the military?" She pshawed him as she turned her head in a bashful manner and waved him off with a big broad smile. "That looks like something my drill instructor might have done. Some of the people in my platoon needed everything spelled out."

Babe wasn't sure what the feeling in his gut was saying. Part of him warmed at the thought he'd gotten two kids off the street, but in his heart, he figured two sets of parents pined for their kids. The right thing to do was find their parents or learn the story. No matter how he painted it, the kids were not his responsibility, only a substantial liability. What was he going to do, turn his grandfather's house into a home for runaway boys? Maybe the boys came from abusive homes, like the kid he saved from the apartment a block from his place only months prior. That bastard got his comeuppance, and Babe didn't lose an iota of sleep. Given the same situation, he'd do it again in a heartbeat. While Ruthie had set some guidelines, what was the end story? He'd talk to Trinity, maybe Trey and Max, the odd couple. What he knew was he didn't want to raise teenage boys.

Trinity found a glass and an open bottle of scotch and poured her man a drink. "Big man, I see that top spinning in your head. Leave it be until Sunday, and we'll have a plan by then. Also, we'll talk to the sassy caretaker; I can already see she has an opinion. All her children are grown, and she has the itch to be a mom again, and frankly, I think that ship has sailed, but maybe not? No decisions today."

WHO'S WHO?

*T*he hospital on Pensacola's main drag was clean and well-staffed, unlike many of the establishments in the area, since the pandemic. Handcuffed to the hospital bed, Tim "Chop" Faraday raised a ruckus, yelling they were holding him against his will. The police were mistaken; they had the wrong guy. He wanted a lawyer.

The nurse entered his room. "Mr. Faraday, you must quiet down; you're upsetting the other patients. You sustained a few injuries; the doctors want to keep you for observation, but it won't be too long." She checked his IV and the monitors. "You've gotten yourself so worked up; your vitals are going crazy." She avoided looking at the restraints and focused on his face, the machinery anywhere but his arm or ankles.

"Lady, is there a cop outside my door?" He tried to appear rational, but the glare of rage broke through and was unsettling. "I'm a vet; I need to be at the VA on Uncle Sam's dime. Tell that fucking pig to come in here; I want to talk to him. I know he's there." She scurried out of the room. The creep was downright scary. At the top of his lungs, he screamed incessantly, "Get me outta here, you bunch of fuckin assholes. Lemme loose. Lemme loose. Fuck you, you fuckin cocksucker. I know you're out there."

The police officer, a forty-something, well-built, clean-cut man, opened the door, followed by the nurse, who had a syringe in her hand. She popped the cap off and, guarded by the officer, injected the IV port. "Good night, Mr. Faraday." Slowly his speech slurred, and his eyes closed to half-mast. He grumbled a few obscenities before fading to silence.

The nurse returned to her station to chart:

0250- Pt. is a 34 y/o white male presenting with extreme agitation and behavior disturbance. Pt. has been escorted via Pensacola police. Pt is in 2-point restraints in the lower extremities bilaterally. Left upper extremity also secured to hospital bed per police request. SN administered Haldol 0.5ml IV site to Left arm. Vital signs 186/98. Pulse rate is 101 bounding. O2 Sat 98% via RA. Respirations 28, however erratic due to outbursts. Unable to obtain any further assessments at this time. Pt was admitted through ED. 0258- SN able to obtain vital signs WNL. Pt. behavior disturbance has improved due to IV medication. SN will continue to monitor q 15 minutes for 1HR.

Once charting was complete and the calamity of noise from Tim Faraday had ceased, Nurse Shelley approached the police officer.

"We brewed a fresh pot if you're interested. I appreciate your help." She pointed to the door of the crazy man's room. "He's a head case. I suppose he'll leave with someone from your department or the jail. I think he needs to be on the psych ward in isolation."

He turned up his palms and shrugged, "Don't know. I just do as I'm told." Easing the tension, he said, "I think I'll take you up on the coffee."

Nurse Shelley put up a finger for him to hold tight, "Be back in a jiff."

From his palatial suite overlooking the Gulf, Javier Garcia, the seemingly civilized capo of a cartel in Cartagena, rehashed the problematic situation caused by Tim Faraday, his favorite helicopter pilot. The twin tag team, Tim and Jon, had proven themselves useful not only running the cocaine and some fentanyl but were spotless when it came to trafficking street kids and the occasional attractive woman for his Chinese constituents. The kids, without contest, were the bigger ticket. No one had the whole story about what took place on the beach. The best he could glean was someone intruded during the transfer, and one of the brothers ended up dying at the hospital and the other in police custody. Nobody was entirely sure of the hows. His man on the inside, an older, almost retired sheriff's deputy, hadn't heard a word other than shots fired near the copter tours, assailants, and possible would-be hostages taken to the hospital. The deputy was readily losing his value.

Even though considerably younger, his most trusted and loyal Lieutenant, Seb, was the closest person to him. He joined his capo, and they looked out at the view. Seb suspected the gears were grinding in his boss' mind. Like Mateo Moreno, Javier came across as a gentle, sophisticated businessman making it hard to imagine the atrocities he'd committed. He had strength in silence, just like Mateo. "Seb, who is in police custody, Tim or Jon? Whichever, I want him out or at least silenced." That meant Seb was to select a handful of sicarios to retrieve whoever the police had or silence him if they couldn't secure him or if Javi's attorney couldn't get him off. "Have the helicopter off the beach; we'll need to set up a new avenue." Javier clasped his hands, then swiftly turned his head to Seb with an exaggerated wink. "You are my most dependable and yet so young." He patted the side of the young man's face.

"You got it." That's all it took. There was something to birds of a feather, his American connections were arrogant, too full of themselves, but he also knew they quaked in their boots when thoughts of his displeasure plagued their minds.

Quite often, Javier would reflect on how Mateo would have handled something. It had been several years since his capo, a childhood friend closer than brothers, had been assassinated. The situation still bothered him. Why had Mateo sent him out on an errand when he had at least thirty men on the compound that he could've sent? Had one of the other people gone, he would've met with the same demise, the target of a massive explosion. Javier should feel grateful but somehow didn't. Perhaps, if he had been there, he might have seen or sensed the bombs and protected Mateo. What he felt were guilt and sadness.

If rumors were true, Delores Moreno, Mat's sister, also now dead, was the one who put the hit on his friend. While beautiful beyond words, ice ran through her veins, and she received just desserts due to her flawed soulless character. *That was one hard-ass, manipulative bitch, but gorgeous and an amazing fuck*, he reflected. She knew how to work her attributes to get her way and control those around her. Delores had probably killed and ordered the murder of more people than he or Mateo ever had. One didn't want to stay too close or too long.

Javier twisted a lime to perfection into his glass and added a pour of sparkling water, dropping the squeezed wedge into his drink. It was now a sit-and-wait proposition. He felt assured Seb would have everything handled.

Trinity twined her legs around Babe's as they lay in bed. "What are the options with those kids? I don't think we can drop them back on the street, not now. How can someone get attached like this in barely a day? You've been with them longer. I know I said it would hold until Sunday, but we gotta at least talk about it, right?" He nodded in answer to her question. She could tell he was weighing the options as he had a faraway gaze. She nudged him a little forcefully, "Hey, you, you thinking about the kids or are you—" He continued with a mesmerized still stare. "Oh, no, you don't." She straddled his body. "Babe, you come back to me."

He grabbed her arms, threw her onto the mattress, and stealthfully rolled out of bed, crouching on the floor as though stalking. He slowly moved onto his stomach, legs spread, balancing on his elbow with the other arm extended slightly. He wiped his eyes with the back of his hand along the knuckles and resumed the position. One hand cupped the illusory item, fingers pointing up as though holding something in his palm, while the fingers of the other hand seemed to grip whatever object he had. She watched, and it hit her; he was hallucinating a weapon in his hands. "Motherfuckers," he growled. Then he seemed to relax but remained in the same position for what felt like fifteen minutes but probably more like five.

Trinity prayed no one in the house heard the racket coming from their room, but she knew they had to have. Her thoughts were, 'Please, nobody knock on the door.' She couldn't fathom what the outcome of such a thing would be. Silently she prayed for God to take away his episodes. 'Wake him, God. Have Mercy on him, please.' The tears streaked her cheeks. She wasn't afraid for herself, although she probably should be fearful. He'd slammed her pretty hard on the mattress. The room was dark; she took a chance and pressed the button on the bedside lamp. Would the light illicit some other reaction or demon? She prayed with her eyes tightly closed. Her heart was beating so hard she could feel it in her ears.

Babe gently stroked her arm and then enveloped her prayerful hands with one of his. "I'm sorry. I'm so sorry. I guess thinking about the boys drugged and bound in the van triggered a thought of children in distress, which brought the memory of a target exercise I used to stimulate my focus. I'd visualize that fucker that blazed through his family. My shots were always true and pinpoint accurate. I guess that's where I went. I'm sorry, Trinity. How loud was I?" She assured him that if he'd been as loud as it felt, Ruthie or one of the boys would have surely knocked, but they didn't. Running through her mind, he seemed to be in a sniper position like she'd seen on TV shows, not standing at a firing range, but she was just grateful the hallucination was over.

As the sun began to rise, Babe went into the yard to do his workout, at least what he could without his weights. His senses were keen, and he could feel someone watching him. It was Reg. "So that's how you stay so strong. Tell me what I need to do to get strong; I know I'm scrawny, but I have faith that I'll grow. My bio dad was six feet tall." Babe was interested. Maybe he wouldn't have to pry too much to get some information, like the questions Trinity had posed, and he had wondered—how the boy ended up on the street.

Babe signaled the kid to join him, starting the workout again, this time including the boy in the exercises. They began with sit-ups; Reg reached twenty-five, with Babe coaxing him onto thirty. "Way to go, Reg. Now pushups." It was a hard count to twenty. "Wanna run with me? You can say no; it's okay." Babe smiled. "No judgment at all, but if you want to, you need to stretch with me." Reg closely followed the big guy's movements shadowing his every stretch. "Ready?" and off they went. It wasn't much of a run for him, but the kid seemed thrilled. They jogged, ran, jogged, ran, and after about a mile at the most, Reg tuckered out. They walked back to the house, which presented the opportunity for the boy to open up to him.

Reg's story was one often told. Dad was military and killed in action, Mom remarried a year later, and she and stepdad had two kids and had no time for him anymore. He felt invisible, and when they did talk, it was to criticize. The boy was small in stature for fourteen, but from the sound of his voice, he hadn't hit puberty; maybe the malnourishment had something to do with that. If he were to take on the two boys, he'd have to go through the proper channels. This was something he needed to confer with Trinity and Ruthie.

Since Glenn wasn't expecting him, it gave him a few days to sort things out with Rune's financial advisor. There were things to consider, like insurance and liability. Did he have to get permission from the court? He needed to brush up on the law and put the shine back on his law degree. Maybe, he should drop them back with their street friends and call it a day, but that didn't feel right, either. The situation he'd created wreaked havoc on him mentally. He was angry, sad, and feeling trapped. *Fuck feelings; they were overrated.*

One of the deputies on duty escorted a forty-something-year-old man dressed in a splashy navy silk suit back to an interrogation room. "Thank you," he graciously said, knowing the deputy would remain by the door and somebody else was on the other side of the window listening to every word, which violated the law, but it was better to play the game.

Tim looked at the stranger, head to toe, with questions in his eyes. "Who are you, and who sent you here?"

The man unbuttoned his jacket as he sat and then opened his briefcase. "I'm Gil Pavalora," and he handed him his card. "I am a friend of a business acquaintance of yours. I understand the charges are kidnapping and intent to distribute narcotics. I can see how the sheriff confused the issue, being that it was your deceased twin brother, my condolences," and he bowed his head reverently, "That was the offending party."

Tim tilted his head and furrowed his brows in confusion. Then, like a flipped light switch, he nodded with a long face, thanked the man for his condolences, and affirmed that his brother had made some mistakes and he was only trying to stop him. The web of lies expanded. Running through Tim's mind were thoughts trying to figure out how it would all work and was it a possibility, anyway. "And, Mr. Pavalora, what happens now? They kept me in the hospital for a few days and then brought me here. I think they're transferring me to Escambia County Corrections later today. That's what I heard."

Gil Pavalora was five-eleven or six feet tall with perfectly coiffed black hair and dark brown eyes. He looked the part of a high-paid attorney, and all Chop could figure was Javier Garcia sent him. If he did get him released, getting in the car with the man was a scary proposition. Odds were it would be a short trip to his death. Maybe it would be better, he considered, if he went to jail; there, he would stand a fighting chance at survival.

Whoever they paid off got him his freedom. According to Pavalora, Javier had things set in motion for him in Tampa, where he could hunt his prey in the city and close by St. Petersburg and Clearwater. Tourism kept the area full of vacationers with wallets of ready cash and credit cards, the perfect lure for runaways and street kids. The moderate temperatures provided a comfortable haven for the homeless. Not as decadent as New Orleans, Tampa was still a gauntlet of pockets to pick and side hustles aplenty. If the area didn't produce as expected, Pavalora said Javier would move him to Miami-Lauderdale, where more powerful and treacherous cartels had laid claim; things could get dicey—a most disturbing thought to the pilot.

Pensacola had been perfect; it drew cargo from New Orleans, Biloxi, Mobile, and further east along the coast of Fort Walton Beach, but he'd screwed that pooch. His obsession with impressing the boss was the story of his doom. If he hadn't taken the bait of the two-bit punk wanting to sell some hot, affluent piece of ass, he would have never had the occasion to walk into Louie's and face of all people, Babe Vicarelli.

One thing he knew firsthand was Captain Vicarelli was no one to fuck with. He'd seen him in combat and knew he had an allegiance like none other for his team and those he considered part of his life. Karma was a bad joke; the one enticing target, perfect for a black market sale, had to be none other than the big guy's lady. While the cartel scared the shit out of him with their brutal, merciless measures of torture, Babe was a different kind of intense creator of nightmares; it was like he reached in and strangled the soul with his righteousness.

In Chop's eyes, Babe was as close to the perfect Marine as humanly possible. His goodness and trustworthiness were legendary—he was an icon. Chop knew while he could pull him limb from limb in a torturous death, he'd also heard the rumors of mind-fucking the enemy into submission. The complete loss of self was far more frightening.

Tim's return to his addict wife and hope of being a dad had long flown out the window. They were better without him anyway. Maybe she'd get clean, and perhaps Jagger might have a chance at life and not descend to a criminal's life. Once, he believed in goodness, but that had been what seemed a lifetime ago. The life-altering impact drugs had on him was terrifying—honor, happiness, love, and a future were mere glimpses from the past. He'd gone the way of the serpent.

In the forefront of his mind, however, was revenge. He needed to avenge his brother's death; certainly, Javier would understand. Gil relayed that New Orleans was off-limits and Tim needed to follow instructions or else. Since Jon, his brother, also his second pair of hands in the drug and trafficking endeavor, was dead, he needed a new sidekick in the hustle. Javier provided a most competent partner, one of his sicarios, or hitmen, Arturo Lozano. It was a directive, period. The choice, so to speak, was play by the rules or die.

Anger seethed within him, but he held his cool and tried to remain level-headed. "Gil, I have one thing to do in New Orleans. It won't take me long. Babe Vicarelli killed my brother, and I need to settle the score; he needs to pay. He's a big fucker with wicked skills, but I know how to leverage the situation. Check with Javier, tell him I need one day, that's all. Call him; I'll talk to him and make him understand." Gil raised one eyebrow and stared at him through soulless eyes but placed the call.

SECRETS, REALLY?

Sunday was upon them in a blink. The boys had settled down, and without one word, Ruthie had taken on the role of mother, caretaker, and enforcer of the household rules. She ran a tight ship. One dyed-in-the-wool obligation was church attendance on Sunday, and not up for debate.

Ruthie's son, Clive, drove his mother and the two cleaned-up kids to services, leaving Trinity and Babe alone in the house. The soothing rain-like sounds from the shower softly invaded her sleep, waking her gently. Shaking the slumber from her head, she entered the bathroom to observe her man. It was quite a show—the rippling muscles and fluid movements, combined with his animal prowess, caused her to pause attentively.

No matter how often she'd seen his body, it was a delight; she figured it would never lose her interest—every muscle bulging and defined in concise ripples. His body art, which she came to learn, was almost like a Marine language in itself, danced along the shifting muscles. "Boy, I love your body. Want company? We gotta be quick, though, because Dad is expecting us for Mass and then the barbeque at Bethany's. Remember?" She had her hair twisted up, held by a giant claw, and swiftly moved into the shower, avoiding the spray. "Move the head so it doesn't sprinkle my hair." He blocked the water from hitting her. "I guess you had your workout this morning. How'd it go? Did you have company or solo?"

Babe smiled down at her and then lifted her onto the shower bench. She leaned down slightly to kiss him. It was always a gamble; would he devour or gently cover her with rosebud kisses? This morning he went for the gusto, kissing her hard, parting her lips, challenging her to a duel of tongues. He grabbed her ass, lifting her against his wanting body. "C'mon, girl; don't hold back." She wrapped her legs around him.

"Take me to the bed, Babe." She moaned through his deep exploring kisses.

She grabbed a towel on the way to the bed, still in his arms, and clutched it to her body. He gently placed her on the bed.

He lay beside her, draping an arm over her abdomen. "Trinity, you've whipped me; all I can think of is pleasing you. Do I satisfy you?" His intense, questioning eyes had a vulnerable, scared little boy hiding amidst the accomplished military man. She wriggled from under his arm and hopped off the bed with a huge grin across her lips.

"And then some." She giggled. "Now, quick into the shower. We gotta get a move on; I'm not going to be late to Mass."

Trinity climbed into the Ford F-250. "This certainly isn't the most ladylike vehicle to get into, Babe Vicarelli." He looked over at her with a one-sided grin. "You know where St. Dominic is? We used to go to Pius, but because most of us, except Mama, Daddy, and Bethany, lived in Lakeview, we all decided on St. Dominic. That's where most of my nieces and nephews go to school, then Mount Carmel or Cabrini High for the girls and Jesuit for the boys. I told you I talk a lot. So, do you know where the church is?" He shook his head no. "I didn't think so. Go like you're going to the house in Lakeview. Parking this monstrous truck might be a problem. If I'd thought about it, we could have parked at the house and walked, but it's too late now—which brings me to your question. Babe, you do just fine in the lover department. I know you've never had a girlfriend, but you're taking to it like a duck to water if you get my drift." She winked with a naughty girl smirk. "Like so until me, you've never had foreplay?" She double-raised her eyebrows in a quick hitch. He swore he could see some pink shining through her beautiful caramel cheeks. "Never?"

He looked straight ahead while driving and tilted his head, weighing an answer. She could see the smile grow on his face, but he stayed silent, feeling a warmth tingle on the tips of his ears. "You know the answer. You're my real first kiss, Trinity. It's never been about anybody's gratification but mine. The working girls don't expect anything; they're working, and the other few that gave it up willingly wanted to get laid, not kissed, groped, just a pure hard-core fuck, and I actually feel accomplished in that department. I've revved more than one engine, of that I'm sure because the same few girls came back for extra helpings." He let out an abbreviated laugh.

She pulled down the visor and applied her makeup, glancing in his direction as his truck bounced in and out of potholes. She fastened an extra button looking down at her chest. A quick tug on her skirt and a touch of lipstick must have ended the primping because she let out an audible sigh.

Babe explained that he attended a Catholic school but didn't remember much about it. "How bout I meet you after church; I'll wait outside. Then, we can go to Bethany's." To him, that sounded like a plausible solution. He had no desire to go to church; as he'd said before, there was no evidence of a loving Creator. He was trying for her, but church?

"Are you kidding me? Hell no, Babe. Your ass will be sitting right next to mine. You're a smart guy; you'll figure it out." Under his breath, he said something about lightning striking the church with him in it. She slowly shook her head. "Big guy, you are who God made you. I'm not asking you to go to confession or anything, but I want you to go to communion. You are Catholic, right?" He shrugged a shoulder. "You went to Catholic school? Have you ever had communion? I'm pretty sure you're Catholic; otherwise, you stay seated during communion. If you sit it out as a lie, I'll find out. What do you have against believing in God?" *Another day, another discussion,* he pondered.

He found a parking spot a couple of blocks down from the church. *Best to stay silent.* He quickly got to the passenger side and helped her out of the truck. She held his hand and gave it a couple of tight squeezes to let him know the discussion was not over.

The entire family gathered in front of the church, including nieces, nephews, and to his surprise, Glenn, who apparently was Bethany's fiancée. Babe found it odd that his boss had never said anything about being engaged to Bethany. Then the question begged, did he take the position in the company working for the family, or did his relationship come after? *The old chicken and the egg, hm.* Her father made his way to Babe and put his hand out. Babe shook hands, and a brief, cordial conversation pursued. There was no doubt they were family; they all had similarities either from their mother or father and unlike many families, they got along and were genuinely happy to see each other. What was the real story behind Trinity working at Louie's, not the hotel?

Fortunately, the Mass wasn't as uncomfortable as he had expected, and he listened to the Sermon or Homily and could relate to some of the things the priest said. The thing of it all was if anyone knew who he really was, they'd usher him out in a heartbeat, spawn of Satan that he was. Then, he started to think of Antoine, her dad. Babe casually looked in the direction of the man, her dad was held captive by every word, and the sincerity on his face was authentic, yet when Babe considered the man, he had a hard time understanding. Maybe this might be a situation that required more reconnaissance.

He liked to think he had a pretty good bullshit-o-meter, and either the dial wasn't working, or the man was genuinely repentant of his sins. What were his sins? Did he erase those who got in his way, or did he pay them off? Thought—in a payoff, who was the sinner, the one offering to pay money to get their way, or the person who accepted money, like a prostitute of sorts? *Business was business, whether it was receiving money to look the other way or selling one's body for monetary gain.* Paying off inspectors could lead to improper building standards and the possibility of someone getting hurt, but if it was just because of the stickler red tape, then, in that case, a bribe was perfectly okay in his book. The rules were there for a reason, but some seemed excessive. Services ended, and they walked hand-in-hand back to the truck.

"So, what'd ya think?" She bounced alongside him. She cocked her head and examined his appearance. "We're gonna stop by Mama's so I can do something with your hair. I don't know why you colored it, and this, she grabbed his longer facial hair. I love your stubbly five o'clock shadow, but this bushy stuff has to go. Doing what you did earlier, I bet if I got close enough, you'd wreak of—"

"Maybe I like that," he chuffed. "I get into your natural scent; it makes me excited just thinking about it." She slapped him on his arm and frowned. "What? I can't help it. I want your scent all over me." Her eyes widened as saucers, and once again, her cheeks took on a pink undertone. By this time, they reached the truck. He helped her into the vehicle. He inhaled deeply. "I savor that aroma." She squealed and said that was enough dirty talk for the day, punctuating it with a hand up and an 'oh, gross' comment.

He walked around the truck, watching her through the windshield. His lips formed a shit-eating grin. As much as she had groped him and whispered sexy suggestions in his ear, this was a first for him throwing her sassiness back at her. He got into the truck, grabbed the back of her neck, and pulled her into an engulfing kiss, sliding his hand up her skirt, going for the gold. She held his face as she returned the intense kiss. She broke away. "Let's go to my Mama's so I can take care of that hair, and if you hold still while I buzz it, I'll take care of something else before the barbeque."

Babe suggested they were closer to her place than her parents; besides, fooling around at her parents would not be cool. Her parents lived in a grand house on Swan Street in Lake Vista. The home was all pomp and circumstance from the outside, but it felt lived in and warmly inviting once inside. He could easily see a house full of kids scampering around, creating havoc and noisy fun with lots of smiles and laughter. It was something he never had, not that he begrudged her for having it.

Trinity pulled him toward the kitchen and pointed to an island barstool. He sat while she ran off to gather the supplies to barber him. Within twenty minutes, she finished. He rubbed his hands over his head. She left the top longer than he usually liked and cropped the underneath and sides. In a manner of speaking, it was a weird high and tight. She combed his wild beard and buzzed it right off.

"Go look. I hope you like it." She led him to a half bath off the kitchen across from the laundry room. "I like it," she said proudly.

"Then, that's all I care about. I told you, shave the whole motherfucker. It's hair." He looked in the mirror, and she'd done a great job. The blond-grey set off the dark shorter new growth, and the cut made for a more sophisticated look than he'd ever sported. "Girl, you missed your calling. Damn, it looks great." She stood taller, shoulders pinned back with hands on her hips, giving her a spunky appearance. "What's that look for?" She pushed past him, shutting the door as she leaned against it. "No, ma'am." She groped his crotch pulling on the zipper of his pants. "Trinity, no." He gave a half-hearted attempt at turning away.

"Just a little love nip, like you haven't done to me? Turn about is—"

"Let's put everything away if we're still going to the barbeque. If not, let's head to my place. I understand it needs straightening." She shook her head and told him Bethany's was still on, and he wasn't getting out of it.

Trinity swept the floor, then set the house alarm, and they left. He started for the truck, but she took his hand, and they walked next door. "What the fuck? Everyone's next door, and you carried on like that? Trinity, not cool." His face was deadpan, not a smile anywhere in sight.

She nudged him in the ribs. "What's wrong witchoo, boy? You just got your nob polished, and you all grumpty-dumpty. You should have a big ol' smile on your face; I saw your knuckles bleach out. Yeah, boy, you were hanging ten riding the wave." The gate whined open. "Babe, pull your shit together, hear me?"

When they rounded the side of the house to the backyard, Bethany ran up, giving them a big hug. She pointed out the bar and asked where their swimsuits were; Babe glanced at her. Another small detail she forgot to mention. Maybe he wasn't boyfriend material. He hated crowds and wasn't into the party scene, while his social butterfly flitted around, dragging him from one person to the other. It must've been the last day to wear white or seer-sucker because almost every man at the shindig wore stripe or linen shorts with pastel shirts. This was not his idea of fun. Perhaps he put off an air of 'leave him the fuck alone' because most people talking with Trinity barely made eye contact with him.

"Hey, Babe," someone tugged on his arm. "I take it this isn't your jam? Mine neither." The sassy redhead with striking blue eyes kept her hand on his arm. "I'm not a party person anymore, but Michael felt he needed to be here." Out the side of her mouth and inconspicuously, she mentioned most of the people at the party were his patients. "You probably don't even remember me, but I'm—"

"Rainie Landry, Dr. Landry's wife. Right?" He threw a half grin in her direction. How could he, or anyone for that matter, forget her?

"Good memory, that's right. Get a drink; I'm drinking club soda with a twist of lime. I've got the perfect place to get out of the way but appear like I'm socializing. Michael gets upset with me when I don't chat," she raised her eyebrows, "with party-goers. Screw that." Babe chuffed and said he understood completely. They grabbed drinks and sat. She had her purse in the seat for one person and her sunhat in the other, staking her claim. "I totally jazz on your name. What a great name."

He sat still, watching her and finding her most amusing. He swore if someone held the girl's hands down, she probably couldn't speak; she punctuated every statement with some sort of hand or arm flailing. He liked her; she was as real as they came. It's not like she was hitting on him or making him feel uncomfortable, just the opposite. They were very much the same—to themselves to let their mind games fuck with them. She had demons, he could feel them, but maybe they were old ones that still lingered in her soul.

"My friend's brother was in the service; I think Navy, but I'm not sure. I understand you were a Marine." He closed his eyes; he hated that expression. "Wait, no; you'll always be a Marine, just not active. Am I close?" He smiled, trying to relax.

"Yes, ma'am. Close enough." The one-sided conversation continued. Where did he serve? How long? What was it like? She knew his tattoos were of significance, but what was it? She'd commented she'd seen other soldiers with tattoos, but his were actually art.

"Marine, not soldier." He half-smiled, "But that's okay, now you know." He observed her movements but kept track of Trinity and her buzzing from one conversation to another.

"Were you like some badass Marine, like in Special Operations? You know, like on TV and in movies? Michael would have made a great Marine. He's so smart and can read people like no one else I know. As kind and gentle as he is, there's a whole different side to him. One nobody sees but the one that's getting the brunt of it." She took a sip of her drink and stared off into space. He knew that distant thousand-yard stare, but where had she gone? He could see a glaze develop over her eyes, invisible tears rolling down her cheeks. He knew those invisible tears; they ripped the soul right out of one's body.

"Rainie, you're not alone in your fight." They stared into each other's eyes. He knew she knew. "A man once asked me if I was a good guy or bad; nonetheless, he bet I was some motherfucker's nightmare, and that's the truth, I am." She answered so was Michael. Maybe he didn't look like a badass, but he didn't think twice when it came to killing someone who hurt her. Babe understood.

"Shit, I can't believe I said that. It's not my usual barbeque or cocktail party conversation. I don't know why I said it, other than I think you get it. Michael talks about his patients, never names; he's so Hippa conscious."

She wobbled her head from side to side. "Perfect Michael, ya know." Her voice trilled in emphasis. "After meeting y'all at Louie's, I kinda put two and two together. I remembered a call from the Noelle family late one night; evidently, one of their girls was in trouble, and I knew it had to be baby girl, well, because she wasn't nicknamed wild child for nothing." She put her hand up as though to pause. Babe was all ears. "Don't get me wrong, friend, I was screwed up six ways from Sunday until just a few years ago."

Trickling through his mind was how he'd told Trinity almost everything and now all the things she'd held back. Was she afraid to tell him? If so, why? Was it a past she didn't want to revisit? He'd be quiet and nod and let Rainie continue her roll. "I understand." He nodded.

"I don't know why I'm babbling so much. Maybe it's because you've probably seen and heard the worst of humanity and won't stand in judgment. I don't know, but I like you Babe. Not many people know, but one of my dead ex-husband's partners abducted me and planned on killing me. He was nuts. It was all over money and lewd office behavior." She closed her eyes, shaking her head as though disgusted by it all." She dropped her voice to a low whisper. "The guy had me in an old derelict fishing camp, but Michael found me and killed the guy. I know, probably shocking, my sweet Michael. That day he was all business and didn't waste a second or a word. Done, crushed windpipe and bullet between the guy's eyes. Of course, it's like some horrible dream to me, but I remember and still have nightmares sometimes." She took another sip of her drink. "Well, there's my skeletons. How about you?"

He set his jaw and stared into space like he had an internal debate in progress. "Too many to count, but I can say no one will ever have to worry about the guy who abducted Trinity again. That's a tale between friends." He held up his drink, and they clinked glasses.

Michael approached them, "So, has my wife been playing the twenty-question game with you? She's quite proficient at it. Anyone who knows her knows she's always one for a question. Rainie's the most curious woman I've ever met. Did she tell you I fell in love with her at first sight? Very true. Not one regret to this day. She's amazing. Nuttier than a fruitcake, I wouldn't have her any other way." Rainie laughed from the pit of her soul. Her laugh was contagious, igniting laughter in anyone around.

"Dr. Landry, your wife is one of the most unique people I've met. Honest to the core." The men exchanged smiles and glances. He knew Mike had heard that statement a thousand times.

"It's Mike, and yes, she's bold, very bold. Don't ask her what she thinks because she'll tell you, like it or not." Michael leaned over and kissed the top of her head. "Rai, have you eaten?" He looked at Babe, "Trying to get her to eat sometimes is a challenge. You need to get something, too. They always have great food at their parties."

Just then, Trinity ran over to him. "Babe, you have to get some of the barbeque, and my brothers have been looking for you." She glanced at Rainie, "Thanks for keeping him occupied. I know he doesn't want to be here. Tell him, Dr. Mike, that my family doesn't bite." Mike looked at the big guy. He knew the score; Rainie would've rather been getting a root canal than to be there, and Babe didn't seem much different.

The afternoon passed, and he managed to speak with everyone at the event. Bethany was the complete opposite of Trinity. She was quiet, demure, and soft-spoken. He spoke briefly with Glenn amidst a circle of other men, some of Trinity's brothers. He revisited the steel girder experience, with Babe being the superhero. Many of the guests commented thankfulness regarding his military service. Men, for some reason, liked to talk about his physique and workout methods. Chance even brought up the new coif. Trinity quickly said she had just given him a haircut and trimmed his beard. *Yeah, and an amazing hummer in your parent's house while everyone gathered next door.* He bet that was something that would quell the party chatter. It pissed him off that she had not been crystal with him, yet he'd opened up about almost everything. If their relationship was going to work, he had to feel confident in her loyalty, and at the present moment, he didn't.

TALK TO ME

7he party was close enough to the end that leaving wasn't rude. Babe hadn't said a word to Trinity except the occasional yes, maybe, or great, and she felt his coolness toward her and had no clue about the change in temperament. He turned on the radio. After about five minutes, she turned it off.

"What's up, Babe? Something has shifted gears, and I'm perplexed." She tilted her head to one side. "Was the barbeque that horrendous? It seemed you and Rainie Landry hit it off just fine. If it were any other woman, I'd probably want to knock the shit out of her, but Rainie is all about her Michael. Everybody else on the planet calls him Mike, but not her; it's always been Michael. So, back to the question, what crawled up your ass?"

Silence. The pregnant pause was deafening. Trinity began to shift in her seat. "How'd you get the nickname Wild Child?" He looked straight ahead.

"Please tell me that's not what your silence is about." He asked her again with a bit of harshness in his tone. "For fuck sake. When I was sixteen, I got pregnant. Bethany hadn't even had sex yet, and here I was, knocked up. It's not like I was easy, but I had the major hots for this guy, one of my brother Antoine's friends. He was over eighteen, which is statutory rape, pointed out by my father. We were smoking dope, cigarettes, drinking, the whole enchilada. My Mama wanted to keep it all hush-hush and went to Mass daily to pray for my soul. Daddy wanted to kill him; no kidding, huh? The long and short of it my body was too young to carry a baby, and I lost the pregnancy, but I had already quit school—can't go to a Catholic high school pregnant. I got my GED and started working with Shep. He was the only one that didn't judge me. He called me his little Wild Child but kept his eyes on me like a hawk. I learned my lesson, and it wasn't until I married Joey that I engaged in sex again. I gave up smoking and drugs, but over the past few years, I do enjoy my wine. Still, to this day, some people refer to me as Wild Child but don't know the freakin' story, and if you don't want to be with me, take your marbles and go home. I am who I am, and I love you, Babe Vicarelli. I hope my body will be strong enough to bear your child one day, but first comes marriage. Question answered?"

Babe felt guilty for all the thoughts that ran rampant through his head, like from when the hooker Candy made a loaded comment. Then, like a lightning strike, he realized it didn't matter if she had been a lady of the night; he loved her. Who was he to judge anyone? Enough said on that, but he wanted her story from birth to the present, and that's what they would talk about when they got to his place.

"I'm sorry for jumping the gun. I realized I knew nothing about your life story; you knew more about me. Was that on purpose, or it just hadn't come up? Watching you today, you're the life of anywhere you go, and I'm like a sullen mistake of humanity. I'm not throwing any pity party; hell no. I've gone through some tough shit, and no matter how hard I try, I'll always be a jarhead, waiting for my next command, like a fucking dog. I don't dance; hell, I didn't know how to kiss. I never had the occasion where I wanted to."

She tapped his shoulder and reminded him that while he was late to the loving game, he excelled with exponential speed. She loved his kisses and everything else about him, concluding that she knew a lot about him, but to her, he was her superhero, not a mistake of humanity. "Babe, be mine forever."

130

Arturo drove to New Orleans as Chop waffled on about Vicarelli, the super Marine. From the description, it was apparent the pilot had held the man in high esteem, but he couldn't let his brother's murder go unanswered. "When I tell you this guy is huge, I'm not kidding. He must be at least six-four or five, maybe even six, built like a brick shithouse. His eyes dart around, and he takes everything in like some fucking computer. He doesn't talk much, but when he does, he doesn't beat around the bush."

The driver listened intently. "Do you want him to understand the situation, or do you just want me to shoot him and be done with it? If he's the bad motherfucker you describe, I see no point in getting into a physical encounter; just pop and be done."

Chop drummed his fingers to the music while he thought. The sicario was right, but he wanted the satisfaction of seeing Babe try to weasel out of it. The only time Chop saw fear in the Marine was over some life-like rubber snake. He wasn't afraid of the Taliban, the weapons, or hand-to-hand combat, but the snake jarred him to the point where he sliced the rubber reptile to pieces in mere milliseconds.

"Here's what we're gonna do. I know where he stays at, so I say, we put a big-ass poisonous snake in the shower. He won't be looking down, and when he finally sees it, or it bites the shit out of him, he'll stumble backward, and we zap him with a shocker thing. That's sure to bring him to the ground, then we restrain him and slowly bleed him out. He'll suffer from the venom. I want him to know it was me. If his little bitch is with him, we can take her as a bonus. She's fine, alright; you'll like her; I think she's Latino with long black hair, big dark eyes, and skin the same color as yours. She's bound to be a hot-blooded woman the way she gyrates behind the bar. I almost had her once, but the dumb fucks that nabbed her were short on smarts. She's the Super Marine's woman."

Arturo listened, and the more he heard, the more he felt like he had some juvenile in the car with him. He didn't have time for stupid head games. His vote was to get rid of the guy quickly and get out of Dodge. He stopped the car for gas, and while Faraday pumped the fuel, Arturo called

Seb. "This crazy motherfucker you got me with is loco, man. It's like I've got some fourteen-year-old girl wanting to get revenge. This is some kinda shit, and I gotta tell ya, I don't like it. Loco, loco, loco. He's gonna get us both killed or arrested."

After filling the tank, Tim got in the car and called a friend. "I need a favor. You got any venomous snakes." Silence. "Yes, I'm serious. No, it can't just look like one. I want the real thing." He listened to whoever was on the phone. "No, I get it. I ain't going in the swamp. Are you fuckin' nuts? I guess look-alike will do, but it's gotta attack. Okay, okay, how much? No, how much? What the fuck, three hundred dollars? Oh, and that's cause we're friends. I'll swing by in a couple hours."

The rest of the ride, the two men barely spoke but listened to the radio. All the music was Spanish, and Arturo sang along to some of them. When they reached New Orleans East, Chop's head was banging from the music. He understood full well that his companion was trigger-happy and deadly. Chop gave instructions to turn onto Chef Menteur Highway, and finally, they arrived at the pet store. He ran in and, within minutes, came out with a writhing sack. "I'll bring you where you want to go, but I'm not down with your plan. I'll wait outside in the car. If you don't show in half an hour, I'll come and put an end to all this drama. Seb said to let you handle your own battles, and that's what I'm gonna do. I can't believe they even let you come here after all the trouble you caused. Javi must think you're good at what you do. Me, I'd have let you rot. You're a whiny little girl, great pilot or not."

"Fuck you." Chop ran down the side alley and crawled into an open window. It was Babe's bedroom. He went into the bathroom and threw the loose sack in the shower. He had a taser gun and hunting knife. He hid in the closet to wait it out.

They pulled into the first spot they could find, four blocks from his apartment. He held her hand back to his apartment with a feeling of contentment that there were no more secrets, well, not many, between them. Babe didn't think he could ever explain his elation when eliminating a threat or piece of shit. She had already said she knew he'd killed other people yet still looked at him as a superhero, not a monster. In his mind, the answer was clear; there was something deeply disturbed about him.

Upon unlocking and opening the door, the sight took him aback. The state of the place, despite the ramshackle of unbelievable magnitude, had a different vibe, like someone else had been there. Something was amiss. Trinity went straight to work in the front room, uprighting the side table and lamps while he headed for the back. Nothing in his bedroom was out of place, only the front room, but someone had been there, and it wasn't from Trinity maneuvering through the bedroom window. No, someone else had been there recently. He was like a dog picking up the scent of another dog.

Babe joined Trinity in the front room, where he'd thrown the sofa, smashed, and scattered things off his desk. One chair was upside down, while the other was merely wood scraps. He could clearly visualize how that had happened; he'd seen a chair in the same condition one other time when he was twelve; Babe used it as a weapon, disabling his abusive father. All his pictures were on the floor, but he remembered setting the stage, creating a horseshoe of photos taken from all corners of the earth. Even his weights were displaced like he'd started a workout but was interrupted.

Trinity scratched her head, dazed by the wreckage. "What in the hell went on in here, Babe?" She scanned the room, imagining the scenario whereby everything was in total disarray. He stayed silent momentarily, conjuring the right words so she didn't think he was a complete psycho. He picked up the pictures one by one, glancing at each and thankful he hadn't broken any. The vision came to him as he quietly narrated the situation to Trinity. He'd taken a shower and walked to the living room naked, making him vulnerable without any barrier between him and the hallucinations. He'd arranged the photos of his teams, daring the demons to reveal themselves, trying to draw the nightmares from hiding. The few bits that made sense, he tried to explain, but the only rationale lay deep inside his twisted mind. There were no words to describe the torment.

The living room retook shape gradually, and everything slotted back in place as though ready for inspection. With a hand on her hip, slowly moving the other arm in a sweeping motion twisting her body, Trinity said, "Boy, if ever you get this wild hair up your ass to call on your demons, I suggest you go somewhere deep in the woods where you can't break everything in your path. I get that you wanted to face your fears, but not like a tidal wave of destruction. Good Gawd, Babe, I'm sweatin' like a grown-ass man working in a warehouse. Heading for the shower, if you don't mind."

He nodded as he reflected on each picture. Several minutes went by when he heard Trinity scream. He dropped the framed photo and jetted to the bathroom. She froze with her back tightly planted against the corner of the shower. She stood motionless, staring ahead into the opposing corner. His jaw dropped, and his eyes widened. Someone had been in his bedroom and left a four-foot snake in his shower. Babe could face almost anything without a tremble, but snakes were sneaky cowards. He knew that if anyone was going to sustain the strike, it was him. He shielded her. "Move slowly out and hand me a towel." He and the snake stared each other down as it raised its head to strike. Just in time, she hung the towel on his outstretched hand, and he threw it over the head. Trinity grabbed one of his shirts and bolted to the door, catching a glimpse of a man coming from the closet. She was out the door before he could react.

As planned, Chop came behind Babe, preoccupied with the snake, and tased him, the barbs sinking into him, harnessing his abilities momentarily. Arturo came from behind and put a gun to the big guy's head. With all his pent-up hate, he glared at Chop, Babe's body still spasming and immobilized.

"Shut up, or I'll shoot your fucking brains out." The Latin-looking man spoke to his companion with a shrug. "The girl got away." Babe felt a needle jab in his neck and faded into unconsciousness. It took every ounce of strength Arturo and Chop had to throw him into the back seat, gag, and restrain him.

Trinity ran inside the first open door, dressed only in one of Babe's shirts and nothing else. "Help. Help," she screamed. The bartender hurdled the bar, yelling for the manager to call the police. It only took moments for her to say she was a Noelle, and things jumped into a frenzy. Within fifteen minutes, two uniforms and Trey walked into the bar.

The detective took one look at Trinity and knew something had happened to Babe. He started to make a call, but she grabbed the phone and called her dad. "Daddy, they got Babe." Trey took the phone and, upon hearing Antoine Noelle's voice, briefly explained what had happened as far as he knew and where they were.

The detective put his arm around her trying to console her. "Breathe, Trinity. What's going on? Someone took Babe? How?"

Her body was quivering, and her words resonated with fear as she unpacked the story. Somebody from the bar put a blanket around her while Trey scribbled in his pocket pad. And then another person grabbed her arm, tending to a gash along her forearm. All she could think was that the man from the closet had cut her. Strangely, she felt no pain, just terror roused by the assault on Babe.

After fifteen minutes, Antoine Sr. walked through the front door flanked by one of her brothers and a sizeable, intimidating man. Trey figured, bodyguard. The trio of men created a wake of gawkers behind them. "Get these people out of here," her dad barked. He looked at the manager, "You're closed until I say, got it?" He looked at his daughter, "Who?" She shrugged but then began to tell the story about the snake, the man in the closet, and then seeing the man from the closet and a dark-haired guy drag Babe into a black car. Through sobs, she said Babe looked dead. "Trinity, you hear me. Your friend is not dead; no one would be that stupid, at least no one from these parts. Pray, Trinity, and while you pray. Tommy, here," pointing to the guerilla standing next to her father, "is gonna take care of the snake, and the detectives will have their people investigate the situation. We'll find your friend, Trinity."

Trey tried to get a word in edgewise, but as long as Antoine Noelle, Sr. was talking, he wasn't about to tell him to shut up. He knew that as quick as her dad had entered, he'd be exiting, and sure enough.

"Daddy," she cried. "Don't leave me."

On his way out the door, he turned back, returned with a kiss to the top of her head, and told Trey to get her to the hospital and Dr. Landry would meet him there. "As soon as you get a lead on this asshole—"

Trey nodded. What else was he going to do? Firstly, the detective needed to be at the crime scene, not taking Trinity to the hospital. He called his captain, who said Max was on his way and he'd manage the scene. He told Trey to kid-glove the Noelles. When Antoine Noelle spoke, it was like the standard order of things came to an abrupt halt, and the rules changed, no questions asked.

"Trey, I gotta go back to the apartment. This is Babe's shirt, and that's all I got on." Trey said he felt certain her father would notify her mother, and they'd bring whatever she needed. He reiterated for her to calm down that Babe could pretty much take care of himself. They took off for Touro. Dr. Landry was waiting for them.

Mike was the kind of man that settled the storm and relaxed everyone. "Trinity, we have to stop meeting this way." He smiled. "Let me look at your arm." Dr. Mike listened to what Trinity was saying while caring for her arm. "So, why do you think this was something to do with a cartel?"

She told him it was a long story, but she was pretty sure. It was like a lightbulb illuminated, and her eyes widened with recollection like words appeared in a bubble over her head. The terror changed to anger. Trinity told Mike about the helicopter pilot Babe knew from being in Afghanistan and that she knew he was bad news, but Babe felt he needed to do a solid for one of his military buddies. She went on to say the whole thing was a cluster and then described the trip to Pensacola, the drug and human trafficking, and how Babe had stopped him. She cited the entire drama to the doctor.

"That's a compelling story. You believe what you're telling me? Have you told all this to the police?" Her eyes cast downward, and she shook her head, admitting she hadn't because she just remembered it, and it fit together like a mosaic. What could they do anyway? He encouraged her to tell everything to Trey. As he taped the last bit of bandage down, Dr. Mike emphasized she let the authorities handle it. She blurted out that Max had met him; he again advised her to tell the police.

"You were right about one thing, gringo; he is one big motherfucker. I don't know how happy Seb will be that we are bringing him back with us. Maybe we should pop and drop him." Chop shook his head no and said that would be too easy; he wanted to make him pay. Arturo shrugged his shoulders. "You a crazy motherfucker."

Their passenger in the back began to stir. With his feet secured together with tape, Babe slammed his legs into the back of the passenger seat, knocking Chop into the dashboard and splitting his forehead open. Arturo pointed a gun at Babe and told him next time he pulled any shit, he would be getting a dirt nap. As soulless as Arturo was, he found the stare from the giant unsettling. Babe lowered his head and focused his eyes upward toward the driver. Arturo referred to the passenger as Diablo and told Chop one more move from the back, and it was over. He could feel the man sucking his soul.

"Arturo, you Colombians are way too superstitious. He's a Marine;

he ain't no Diablo." Chop held a rag against his head, trying to stop the bleeding. "You pick up the taser gun?" Arturo shook his head. "Fuck! Now the cops can find me, ya know, DNA and shit. Seb will get my back on that; you say they got their hands up all the five-o and politicians like fucking puppets." Arturo gave him a sideways glance. He didn't like Americans, especially not this bozo. "I gotta say, he moved away from the snake pretty damn fast; I told ya he don't like them. He ain't afraid of nothin', but one time he told me he didn't like snakes." He pointed to his temple, "See, I don't forget stuff. I remember."

SHOE ON THE OTHER FOOT

*M*ichael thought about the conversation the whole way back home. The barbeque at Bethany and Glenn's was a necessary social function for him to attend. Even with the rolling of her eyes and disgruntled expressions, he knew his wife would be the woman she needed to be. He remembered her touting, "I get it, Michael; I guess we'll go for a while, but I'm not going to have fun; I know that already." On the way home, she had been a chatterbox about the Marine, what a nice guy he was, and that he was perfect for precious Trinity.

He shook his head, thinking about what the conversation with Trinity might conjure in Rainie's head. With a propensity for getting involved in matters that were not her concern, he feared she might obsess over the cartel tidbit. It had been several years since she went through her misfortune with the cartel, a nightmare and a half. She'd know, however, if he withheld it from her.

Michael pressed a number on his cell. The once Spanish lilt, soft and sophisticated, was now an exuberant French-laced voice that reverberated around the car. "Ah, Mike. How are you? It is good to hear you. What do I owe the pleasure of this call?"

William LaSalle, once Mateo Moreno, was the head of a powerful Colombian cartel until he drastically changed his life for a less complicated, more peaceful way of living. Mike, the surgeon that sculpted the new face, was one of four people that knew his original identity. Although they didn't discuss it, Mike figured the man had a couple of ties here and there under the auspices of a trusted lifelong friend, Noir. He would take William's true identity to his grave.

According to all records, Mateo Moreno died in a ferocious explosion on his compound. This orchestration was of his own creation and freed him from a life he wanted to leave unencumbered. Death was the only way his family and loved ones could live a normal life without threat. Mike had created a new face through three operations forming the person of William LaSalle, a Frenchman from Quebec who occasionally visited Louisiana, staying in the French Quarter apartment owned by Dr. Landry.

"Are you in Louisiana for Labor Day?" Michael inquired.

"Yes."

"Usual, nine o'clock? I know Rai will want to see you." They often would meet at Mike's French Quarter residence, but if he mentioned Rainie, they'd connect in the Landry's pool house. They ended the call.

Rainie opened the kitchen door with a look of concern and watched as Michael pulled into the driveway of their Stella Street home. "Is Trinity okay, Michael? What happened?" He brushed by with a quick kiss, hardly stopping. *Unusual*, she thought.

"She needed stitches, a cut on her arm. Easy." He didn't look at her but busied himself looking in the fridge.

"Michael, are you hungry again? We just ate at the barbeque; you're avoiding me. Spill it, buster." She stood, eyes transfixed on him, waiting impatiently for an answer. No answer, so she moved into the open fridge door blocking his view. "Well?" He kissed the top of her head but didn't answer. Rainie shook her head and walked off in a huff. "Whatever, Michael."

Laughing to himself, he wanted to see how long she could ignore him. Odds were the most would be five minutes. She was such a curious woman, and he knew her like the back of his hand. Her endless question-and-answer game was part of her essence. He opened a bottle of water and grinned at her. Annoyed, she turned away from him.

Michael brought his water into the family room, and she followed on his heels. "Where are the kids?" he asked as he rested his feet on the ottoman. "William is coming over tonight," he said in passing, knowing it would raise her curiosity until she couldn't hold back any longer.

Rainie pushed his feet off of the ottoman and sat. "William? Why? I mean, it'll be great to see him, but I can tell something is going on, Michael. You're all cagey." Michael masterfully told Trinity's story. She held onto every word, and when he mentioned cartel, she put her hand to her lips and feared painted her face a ghostly white. "Babe's a big guy with a lot of training; I hope you assured Trinity he'd be fine."

He guzzled the last swallows of water as she saw his expression draw to one of concern. "Rai, the guy's indeed trained and strong, and if it were hand-to-hand combat or weapon against a weapon, Babe would come out on top, no doubt. But drugged, waking in a strange place surrounded by the cartel, that's a whole different arena. William might have a suggestion or two.

Babe's mind ticked over and over. The regrets he had for getting involved with Chop's bullshit were mammoth. It would be game over if he could get his hands on either man. His seething went to the highest pinnacle. *Okay, Trinity, where's your God?* He questioned in his mind. If there was a God, He better show up big, like a fucking earthquake or parting of the seas. He wasn't afraid of dying or torture; hell, he'd been tortured as a boot and through each phase in the Corps. Each wrung he climbed got meaner, tougher, and more intense. That was the plan, to weed out those that couldn't take it, and he could take whatever they threw his way.

Most people didn't learn about survival at the tender age of twelve when all kids should have been doing was making friends and playing. Babe was more than prepared for interrogation and withstanding pain. What a chicken shit way, putting a fucking snake in the shower. His thoughts rambled—*Trinity got away. That's all that matters.* Babe focused on the situation and weighed the scenarios. The one advantage he might have would be that Chop didn't want his death to be quick; he wanted to savor the moment and relish Babe's pain and fear, which didn't exist—*dumb fuck.* That might provide an opportunity.

The snake dislike arose from a ten-day rotation in the Kandahar province of Afghanistan. It was something they did to lessen the nighttime boredom. They'd hunt with knives and flashlights for the highly venomous saw-scaled vipers or any snake they might stumble upon. The saying that snakes are more afraid of people than people are of them was bullshit when it came to those vipers. Before his very eyes, he watched Marshall struck by the slithering creature with immense speed without warning and latched on to Marshall, a five-foot-nine bull of solid muscle. Babe's otherwise fearless nature developed a dent in the armor. That was the last nighttime hunt he participated in, and from that point, he stayed clear of snakes. If he happened on one, he could slice and dice it inside a second. Having one in his shower, where he found his sanctuary, was an abomination. *Fucking Chop, payback is gonna be a motherfucker.*

If they hadn't been trafficking kids and women for the cartel but working a nine-to-five job like a regular stiff, none of the bad things would have happened. Like they say, mess with the bull; sometimes, you get the horns. Babe didn't look for trouble; it came to him uninvited. Just when he thought life might be throwing him a crumb of goodness, instead, it was a shit sandwich.

"Ya know, Vic, if you'd walked away like I told you and let me do my business, none of this woulda happened. But, no, you are a self-righteous prick; you killed my brother, and now the writing is on the wall—played with the wrong set of motherfuckers. I warned you." Silence from the back seat. Babe wanted to say no, but none of that mattered.

The driver and the pilot exchanged differences in opinion. The driver, a sicario for the cartel, suggested going off-road and dragging him behind the car; that way, they could watch him suffer and die, but Chop wanted to be the one to inflict the hurt. "You don't get it, helo guy, Seb is gonna be pissed, and Javier, shit, he might just kill you too for bringing him into your fuck-up. I think you been doing too much of the dope, and you're loco. You don't know these people. I've grown up all my life with their ways. They don't want no trouble, just make their money and not be bothered. I think you're opening a can of shit that can't be closed." He turned up the music drumming his thumbs on the steering wheel and attempting to sing.

Chop leaned forward and turned off the music. "I may not be all Spictacular like you, but I been working with them for a couple of years, and they like the money I've made them. I'm the best at getting a bird in and out of trouble. I got medals for my service, steel balls, and can get in and out in a flash. Change the fuckin' station; I hate that la bamba shit." The driver turned the volume up louder.

Babe stilled his mind and focused on what he could control.

Trinity was beyond consoling. She knew the situation was dire and wasn't sure how Babe could possibly get out of it. Even though her father had said he was going to be okay, she knew that probably wasn't the truth. They brought her back to their house. The second she was inside, thoughts of earlier that day popped into her mind. She remembered being with him in the powder room and how uncomfortable he had been at first. She felt a slight tickle in her stomach. She visualized the whiteness in his knuckles as he gripped the vanity. Even though it was faint, she felt his knees buckle a smidge.

The fact that he had mainly been with working girls, as he called them, he treated everyone with respect. Was it insecurity or the tightly woven cocoon his father had caused around his emotions as a boy? Whatever the reason, it blew her mind that a man could be in his mid-thirties and never have fallen in love or had a steady girlfriend. Her man was most gifted in the making love department and all sexual practices, although he did not have the experience; the whole thing floored her. Babe was one of a kind and hers. It was a forever kind of love and one she wasn't prepared to lose. She collapsed on the floor in a heap, drawing her knees to her chest burying her head. The tears flowed in a steady stream, her shoulder hitching with the sobs. Her heart was breaking. What were those people doing to him? How could he possibly come out okay?

She knew from the beginning that the helicopter pilot was a piece of shit and couldn't fathom how Babe could have ever given him the time of day. For being an ace at character assessment, why couldn't he see it with the creep? Was he distracted when it came to those he served with?

"Oh, Dawlin'," her mother touched the top of her hair. "You come on, Trinity. Find your faith, honey. Cryin' and frettin' won't do any good. Rather than fall to the floor in hopelessness, get on your knees and pray. I know your daddy is doing what he can, but it's truly in the hands of God."

Even though her tiny body spasmed as she tried to stop the hysteria, Trinity told her mother about the whole incident, starting from when the helicopter pilot walked into Louie's for the very first time. She explained that Babe was one of those Marines that they sent on the most dangerous missions and that he'd seen all kinds of horrors. "He's been in war and killed people, but to me, he's a superhero." She talked for over an hour, the two of them sitting on the floor. "Mama, I don't think I can live without him. What if something happens? How will I know? Daddy says he'll be fine, but what if?"

"Let's get off this hard floor. Trinity, you need to pray. Just keep on praying and praying." Her mother looked away, then took Trinity's hand and walked with her into the living room. "Sit." Her mother walked out

144

of the room and then came back with a Rosary. "This was blessed by the Pope many years ago. When your father was just starting in business, a couple of mobster-like people tried to make him do things, bad things on the construction sites. When he said he wouldn't, they took him. I called the police when he didn't come home, and they said there wasn't anything they could do. I don't know how many hours they had him; the police suggested that he probably ran off with someone. Trinity," she held both her hands and looked into her daughter's eyes, "I knew they'd taken my Antoine. Days went by, no word, nothing.

"I knew they killed him. For hours I knelt by my bed, saying the Rosary over and over, asking that Mother Mary give me the strength I needed. Remember, honey, She watched Her Son, after being beaten, flogged, tortured to within an inch of His life, get nailed and hung on the cross, the Son of God, for our sins. She knows our pain and listens to our prayers. So, you pray, Trinity. Pray for your man and strength." Her mother handed her the rosary.

Rainie watched as a truck pulled into their driveway. She could see the silhouette of a man getting out and making his way to the poolhouse. Michael was already waiting for William; she joined them. As she walked out the door, he turned, "Hello, my friend." He opened his arms; she hugged him. Michael opened the door for them to enter.

After fifteen minutes of pleasantries, the man spoke. "I see you are troubled, Mike. Can I be of assistance?" William sat on the couch and patted next to him for Rainie to sit. Michael handed him a glass of wine and Rainie a bottle of water and then sat across from the man.

Michael ran his hand through his hair. "I don't know if you can help, but maybe you might have some advice on how I can handle something." Between Rainie and Michael, they explained the story of Babe. More animated than usual, her hands were going a mile a minute, and her face took on exaggerated expressions. William listened attentively as the couple filled in details as they remembered about the Marine. He nodded as they spoke.

William sat silently; they could see the wheels as they turned in his head. "Let me see if Noir can make an impression. So, you say this man worked out of Pensacola? The last I knew, it was part of the New Orleans operation run by Javier Garcia. It was a small part of my business, a crumb I shared with my sister." He crossed himself, kissed his crucifix, and pointed upward. "I am so grateful to be out of the fray. The drugs have gotten more deadly, and I never approved of human trafficking, and now it's multiplied; hundreds of thousands of children, even your wealthy moguls, are involved in the States, yes. That is something for the animals in the Middle East, those with no soul. If you would excuse me for a moment?" He took his phone out and stepped outside. Five minutes went by, and he returned. "I will know something tonight or tomorrow."

Rainie and Michael knew not to ask any questions. The visit lasted another hour as they caught up on his son and their five children. The bond Michael had with William was strong. It ended with an agreement that he and Mike would meet at the French Quarter apartment the following morning for breakfast if William had any news.

The car entered old Pensacola, stopped at a warehouse, and the driver blew the horn. A garage door rolled up with the typical whines and metallic crunching. They backed inside. Three men waited outside the door of a private office off the rest of the building, which housed stolen cars, automobile parts, and mechanics tools—an illegal operation, as a best guess. Behind the glass window, facing the warehouse, the office appeared dark and uninhabited. Arturo pointed the gun at Babe and told him to get out. Still laid out across the entire backseat, he feigned difficulty righting himself. Arturo reached in hesitantly and strained to pull Babe from the back seat. The big man could have made this plight easier but wasn't expending any effort to assist. Tim went to cut the tape securing his ankles. "Fucktard, what the hell are you doing? Leave him restrained as much as possible until Seb tells us what to do." He looked in the direction of the three men huddled in conversation. Seb, the man on the left, pointed to a metal chair, indicating they sit the big man. Babe watched their every move. "Seb," Arturo interrupted, "This is Diablo I told you about."

The tallest of the three men had his back turned to them. Looking at him, Babe surmised he was the man in charge, wanting to keep his identity a mystery. *Whatever, dead men don't talk; maybe my number's not up,* passed through his mind. The man's voice was low and sounded Spanish from what little he could hear. Tim approached the man, who signaled him to back away by extending his arm in a harsh deliberate movement keeping his hand balled in a fist. The pilot stopped dead in his tracks. Babe detected a tremble in Chop's body. Was it withdrawal, the need for drugs, or being scared shitless? His best guess was the latter. Babe noticed a slight movement from the darkened office, like a shadow. No one else seemed to notice the motion unless the man with his back turned to them saw the same thing. Was he communicating with the person in the office? Questions. The whole thing was curious.

Two shots from a silencer penetrated the glass and felled the man flanking the right of the unidentified man, as well as Arturo. Not wounded—dead. With two of the men out of the picture, this left the man with his back turned, the person they referred to as Seb, Tim, and the mystery person in the office. Babe silently observed. The tape securing his wrists had worn thin and buckled away from his sweaty skin. Maybe after another twenty minutes, he could have stretched the cheap crinkled tape so it was weak enough to break. Had the person in the office or any of the men wanted to kill him, he would've already been dead. The man facing toward the window stood easily six foot two, maybe taller. He had broad shoulders and jet-black hair, but the suit didn't seem to pull tightly over muscles. He had no idea what kind of game these people were playing or what they expected of him.

Babe noticed the man's shoulders drop slightly. *He's lowered his guard,* the Marine thought. Just minuscule changes in posture could signal an opponent's weaknesses or readiness, but what weapons did he have hidden beneath his jacket or at his ankle?

The man turned decisively. His voice was velvety smooth as he spoke. He was older than Babe anticipated, perhaps in his late forties or early fifties. "Captain Vicarelli, I have a proposition. Your loyalty to me for your life?"

Babe made eye contact and, without inflection, responded, "Loyalty? I don't know you. As far as my life, sir, no one gives a fuck. You speak in riddles."

"Captain, your life is valuable to people of importance and influence." He approached slowly and calculated. "I understand you killed this man's brother," he pointed to Tim. "I also know he wants to avenge and retaliate, but you are too valuable if you will commit loyalty to me."

The light switched on, illuminating the inside of the office. Commander Deary stood on the other side of the window. Babe reiterated. "As I said, I don't know you to state my loyalty. Also, I won't participate in drug or human trafficking, and I won't be anyone's hitman. If that's what you are looking for, then you might as well kill me now."

The man looked at the ground, then back through the window at Commander Deary, landing his eyes on the Marine. He walked behind Babe, drew a knife, and cut the tape, freeing his hands. Rolling his shoulders and stretching his neck, Babe grunted with the stretches. To his surprise, the man handed him the blade and told him to cut the tape at his ankles. Babe couldn't help but think it was a bold move on the man's part. He could've easily killed him and used the man's body as a shield for the shots that were bound to follow. No, there was an edge to the man in the black suit. With a flip of his wrist, the tape split in half at his ankles. Babe handed the knife back, and the man shrugged and said to keep it. The puzzle was scattered, and none of the pieces connected. "What am I doing here? What is it that you want from me?" The whole situation felt surreal and was throwing him off balance. He liked facts, cold, hard, definitive, not some up-in-the-air whimsical fantasy or game.

"I need protection for a meeting where I know the person guarding me is loyal. Just one meeting and you can return to your home. I will provide your transportation and guarantee your safety until you return. The meeting is in a few days, and until then, you will lack nothing."

"Are you anticipating trouble?" Babe asked.

"The man I am meeting has assured my safety. We—" he stopped to formulate or translate the right words. "We are in the same business. He says he merely wants to speak, but I know nothing good about this man. I want to, as you would say, hedge my bets. You would be part of a two-man team. The other man is a specimen with skills such as yourself. He is trustworthy, and I am told you are a trustworthy individual." Babe looked at the Commander, who closed his eyes with a slight nod. *What the fuck is the Commander doing with the cartel? Does not make sense. Fucking weird.*

"And I go home, no strings attached?" Babe asked, and the man nodded.

"I do not know the future, Captain, but there may or may not come a time when I need protection for another meeting. I will compensate you well, but your life is your life. You shall return to your girlfriend, and your employment and life will not change. Is there anything I can do for you or that you want as of this moment? Please consider my request. I have no desire to kill you, but we both know I will." The man turned and started walking away. The Commander subtly affirmed that his Marine would be at the meeting. What the man was asking wasn't out of his wheelhouse. He wasn't planning on going in guns blazing, but if the person he was to meet crossed the line, Babe had no trouble setting it straight. *Hm. Bodyguard.* Babe stood stretching the length of his body, ridding the cramped weariness of riding bound in a back seat.

"I have one thing I feel I need to do. No matter how badly I want to, I won't kill your pilot. I give you my word; I will not kill or permanently maim him as long he stays away from me and those I love." The man nodded as though not bothered.

Babe approached Tim, who was trying to put space or objects between them, running behind a car, and then an engine. He began whimpering and begging. When Babe reached within feet of him, Tim lunged forward, punching him in the face and kicking toward his groin. Exasperated by the weak attempt of the pilot and fed up by the whole ordeal, Babe grabbed one of his flailing arms and ripped his sleeve off his shirt while buckling his legs so he had Tim down flat with his knee on his chest, subduing him. He pressed the knife tip against the pilot's bicep and cut out the two Marine tattoos on his arm. "You do not deserve the right to bear these. Stay the fuck away from me and anyone in my life, or I will kill you." He looked at the man in the black suit, "And that's a promise."

AN UNFAIR MATCH

*B*abe slid into the passenger seat, acutely aware that the nameless man in the black suit was sitting behind him. Tim, with his bloodied arm, was behind Seb, the man driving the car.

"What does Commander Deary have to do with all of this?" The Marine asked. It bothered him to no end that the man he admired was involved with the cartel. Babe knew politics and war made for strange bedfellows, but this was beyond the scope. The Commander had been a cornerstone in the Corps, held in high esteem, but what of all this? It was too much and too weighty on his mind. Maybe Trinity had made him soft, and perhaps he wouldn't have cared a year before, but he knew that wasn't the truth; it would have wreaked havoc in his mind. "And by the way, who the fuck are you? I know you're somebody of importance," paraphrasing the man's earlier words to him.

He heard a brief rumble of amusement. "I'm Javier Garcia." He paused for a few minutes. "Six, maybe seven years back, my capo and childhood friend, Mateo Moreno, assisted your Commander Deary. Several of his men were held captive under falsehoods; Mat liberated and returned them. I know not the fine details, only the broad strokes. In appreciation, the military man said that if ever he needed outside, meaning American, discreet assistance, to call him. When talks started about a potential meeting with my adversary, an untrustworthy man of great dishonor, I wanted someone of substance, not on anyone's payroll, to have my back. That is hard to find in Colombia. I had one man, but I wanted two, so I called.

151

I do not believe in coincidence. When I discovered that a certain former Marine single-handedly had compromised our New Orleans operation, I recovered your name after a relentless pursuit. I took the Commander's pulse on you and learned about your character; in doing so, it came to light that you were a favored son, so to speak, of Mat's military contact. While your involvement interrupted an extremely lucrative business, I also learned your worth. Commander Deary said you would likely not agree and prefer death unless you saw his face." That made sense of sorts to Babe.

Babe pondered his next question. Did he give a shit? "I get what you're saying. Deary is a good man. What I can't figure out is why you keep a junkie for a pilot? He is one lying sack of shit, and the less I have to do with him, the better for everyone." There was silence in the vehicle. They passed the place where the copter tours had been.

In a calm, smooth voice, he answered. "I keep Tim around because he is a fine helicopter pilot, and I have heard stories of combat heroism that have amused my associates. My business, however, has other pilots, and another reckless decision, will make him surplus to requirements." Babe watched the scenery as they approached the Holiday Inn Beach Resort, processing Mr. Javier Garcia's last comment. Reading between the lines, it wouldn't be long before the pilot would step out of line.

Babe cleared his throat. "I will have your back and, not to boast, I am usually one of good judgment regarding tenuous situations and will not hesitate to move you out if I feel an impending danger. If I begin to move you, I insist that you comply for the safety of your and my life. Do you understand my meaning, sir? I will also consider it my duty to protect the other security man as well." The car turned onto the resort.

After a week there, Javier's entourage, including Babe, boarded a private jet for Miami, where he guessed he'd meet the other security guy.

It was the morning after they met with William LaSalle in the pool house.

Michael felt a vibration in his pocket. After tending to his patient, he checked his phone and saw he'd missed a call from William. He returned the call.

"Good morning, Mike. I hope all is well. It appears that Noir is soon to meet with your Marine friend. He and Noir will be acting as security for Javier Garcia. There is a meeting regarding business in Miami. Currently, Donatello Vargas has a stronghold, but you see, securing Miami is like juggling torches. Quite often, one gets burned. Perhaps it paints my picture more clearly. What do you say? There is no honor among thieves? If your friend is the warrior you described, combining the two will be a force. Javi learned well, surround yourself with the best; then you look like the strength, but, my friend, it is an illusion created by those you chose." If Michael wasn't mistaken, he thought he heard a waver in the man's voice. Even though William had a lovely wife and son, somewhere, he had to miss the old life or at least some of the people. "Worry not. Javier has a reputation for being cruel, but I assure you, he rewards loyalty. Business can be brutal, can it not? The timeline was fuzzy; is that the word for not exact?" Mike answered yes with a slight chuckle. "Until the next time, my friend, kiss your wife for me. Perhaps we will visit for the Thanksgiving Feast. Be well, Mike." The call ended.

Decision time—call Rainie or not? Call Trinity or not? What would he even say to Trinity? How could he explain how he obtained the information? He was already five minutes late for his next patient; the calling would have to wait. One thing settled his mind if Babe had teamed up with Noir, woe-betide Mr. Vargas if he tried to break the rules. He felt better about the situation, although not knowing a timeline would be frightening and frustrating to Trinity. He couldn't or wouldn't tell her how he knew the situation and perhaps not give full detail, just that he was safe and was carrying out an order. She would understand—words such as 'following orders' sounded like Babe expressions.

Her bedroom in her parent's house was the same as her teenage years. She lay on the bed, hugging a pillow, still with the occasional muffled sob. How often had she been in the same position looking out at the next-door neighbor's pool with gentle sobs? Trinity cried when she found out she was pregnant and cried even harder when she miscarried, but Babe's situation was a different thing. Uncertainty and fear were the hallmarks of Babe's abduction, and she knew these were bad people. Stop the world I want to get off were the last words out of her mouth, and so it was. She stepped away from everything—no Louie's, no going out or shopping. She prayed the Rosary on her knees and lying in bed, so much so that she would fall asleep mouthing the words only to wake from slumber, bead still in hand.

It had been over a month since the abduction, and she had not heard anything. Her father knew nothing or said he didn't. She believed him. Her days were consumed by lingering in bed or sitting in a pew at St. Dominic's. Trinity had cut herself off from everything and everyone. Then, the questions began. How did she get so close to another man? She swore off relationships after the misstep of marrying Joey. Trinity had a stable of lovely men that she would occasionally date for dinner and maybe a tumble in the sack, but no one she connected with emotionally.

Babe was different, and despite the craziness of his inner demons, she loved him. He was as pure a person as she'd ever met. People might conjure purity with thoughts of innocence, goodness, and piousness, but his probity came from inexperience. He hadn't learned the head games involved with dating and socializing. His quiet nature did not equate to uncaring; he had an open heart, even though he claimed he had always been incapable of emotion, even given that undocumented diagnosis by professionals. They didn't know him or understand him. Babe was the real deal, one hundred percent genuine.

With a light tap on the door, her mother stood waiting for an answer."Dawlin', you need to come out of your room. It's not doing anyone any good for you to stay sullen and locked up in your room all day.

Take Gunner to the dog park or go tell the gang at Louie's hello. They're all missing you."

"Mama, come in. Gunn is just fine in bed with me. He gets me." She ruffled his fur. Everyone had noticed the dog's depression. He had sadness in his eyes and looked up, eager to see Babe's face every time the door opened, but he laid his head down when it was just another person. Trinity bet Gunner longed and reminisced about running with Babe to work, all the men at the construction site giving him treats. Maybe that's where she'd go; at least it would smell like Babe. Sliding her legs off the bed prompted a smile from her mother. "That's my girl." She smiled, even though it had an emptiness to it. "Are you going to see Shep? That busser, Sean Finnegan, has been taking all your shifts, but I bet the clientele aren't as enamored by his smile. They miss you, sweetie."

Trinity closed her eyes briefly, then looked at her mom, answering with a thankful upward turn of her lips. "Maybe." She untied the silk scarf off her head. "Time to shampoo this mop and seek the voices of the living. I've taken your advice about saying the Rosary. It gives me hope; still no peace, but hope is a step in the right direction." She pulled a brightly colored floral blouse and jean shorts from the dresser. She stopped by the bathroom door. "Mama, Daddy says he has no idea who took Babe or where he is. Do you believe him?" Her mother pursed her lips and nodded. There wasn't the slightest air of doubt in her face. Trinity knew her father had questionable contacts but felt secure knowing if anyone could find out, it would be the people in his network.

She shut the door after entering the bathroom and turned on the shower, which brought forth intimate memories. She leaned back under the spray and let it beat on her head, neck, and shoulders. In her mind's eye, she could envision her massive lover looking down at her with love and lust in his eyes. She smiled, thinking how she'd been his first for so many things, and it was hard to comprehend that such a specimen had never had a girlfriend or partook in romance. His touch was so gentle and curious. She wanted Babe home and safe. What if they killed him? How

155

would she even know? Was she desiring and pining for a man that was already dead? "This isn't healthy." She dried off, dressed, and headed for the construction site.

It had already been over a month since his abduction, and not that the accommodations or treatment had been shabby; his heart longed for Trinity. Thoughts flooded his mind. *How long would she wait for him? How could he get word to her that he was okay, merely detained?* Had he not given his word to Javier, he'd have fled, grabbed Trinity, and the two would head to parts unknown if they didn't kill her first as retribution for his disloyalty. The supposed meeting was pushed back too many times for his liking, and hanging in a hotel room, albeit in an elegant setting, was not his idea of a good time.

He'd finally met Noir, who was equal in size. Since they met, they'd exchanged maybe fifteen minutes of conversation, if that. They were quite a pair of bookends, massive, strong, perceptive, alert, and painfully silent. As far as Babe was concerned, that was fine with him. He'd never been one for idle small talk. They were on a first-name basis, neither knowing the other's last name, but he felt comfortable knowing Noir would equally have his back. Between the two, Javier was well-protected. They were there to do a job and nothing more; however, they both found solace in the weight room. When Babe felt like running on the beach, he always had a partner. The other big man matched him pace for pace. It was plain to see Javier had more trust for Noir; Babe didn't hold a grudge; if it were his meeting and his inner circle, he'd feel the same.

The phone in Babe's room rang at the same time as the adjoining room. The men had two hours to prepare and eat; then, it would be protective duty. The hotel delivered room service to Noir's room. "Food's here," he announced to Babe.

"Will Mr. Garcia provide us with weapons?" He felt sure the other security would be armed to the teeth. He slipped a fork and knife into his sock. Javier had provided him with more clothes than he owned at home. He had offered female company, but Babe declined. Whatever stimulation or pleasure Babe desired was encapsulated in his memories of moments with Trinity. He was there for a purpose and didn't need any distractions. The sooner they completed the job, the sooner he'd be back in the arms of his woman.

"Yes, but don't be surprised if you are relieved of them." Noir was matter of fact.

"Well, they'll get a fight from me if they don't surrender theirs first. You?" Babe asked.

"I always have a knife." He demonstrated that his belt buckle separated into a knife. Babe raised his eyebrows, impressed by the stealthy knife.

"I like that, but like they say, don't bring a knife to a gunfight. So, Garcia's gonna give us weapons?"

Noir told him the meeting would go without incident. Afterward, on the way back to the airport, it would be a different thing altogether, in which case they'd all have firepower and the vehicles equipped with bulletproof windows. Their people were already onboard the jet, so there was no funny business. It was the most the two men had spoken in their entire time together. "Babe, I'm pretty astute, but if you feel something going down, I'll follow your lead—"

"As will I if you get the vibe first."

They met in Javier's suite, where he explained they were meeting in a jet hangar; both parties would have their aircraft waiting. Babe thought, *Odd. So no ride to the airport after the meeting. When were they planning the hit?* The Miami head guy pre-arranged everything, making Babe skeptical and leery of the meeting. If he'd known before, he'd have done some reconnaissance, probably accompanied by Noir. The thing they didn't get was he gave his word, and to Babe, that was his bond. Alarms sounded in his head. *What were they up against?* It felt like the decks were stacked against them, which wasn't how he liked a precarious situation.

"Sir, I don't like the plan. It smells of an ambush. Give me the address, and let me go ahead of you; I give my word I won't ditch on you. You've given him the upper hand, sir, which stacks the odds in his favor. Keep Noir with you, and I'll meet you before you head into the hangar." From everything Commander Deary had told Javier, this Marine's word was solid as truth.

"We have men already there, soldier. I've done this before. I need you to make sure I am protected once inside the building."

Babe commented with a more determined tone. "Be that as it may, drop me a few blocks ahead and give me time to scour the place before you arrive. My gut tells me they will attempt an assassination before you even enter the building. Trust my instinct, sir." Javier listened to the severity in his voice and reluctantly agreed. "I promise I'll be with you when you walk into the hangar. Do you have a telescope mirror I can pass under the cars?" Javier tipped his head to the side, answering no and that his people had been with the cars. Babe wasn't satisfied.

Comments went back and forth between the men, Javier warning that if Babe skipped on him, he would hunt him down and kill everyone he loved. He knew precisely where his bartender girlfriend lived and worked and didn't care that her father was part of the New Orleans mob. Babe nodded in agreement. They went down to the awaiting cars. Javier and Noir started to get in the back seat of the middle car. Babe stopped them, removed his jacket, and slid beneath the car.

After a couple of minutes, he emerged and shook his head. "You're not riding in this one, sir." He moved to the first car, rolled under it for a minute or two, and rolled out. "Not this one either, sir." Then he proceeded to the third car. A man he didn't recognize was sitting in the furthest seat in the back. Babe leaned in and pulled the man by the scruff of his neck out of the vehicle. The man had his phone already pulled out and quickly punched numbers. The Marine grabbed it and crushed it under his foot while Noir ran a blade across the man's throat, then threw the dead body into the back seat.

He hailed the hotel's transport vehicle. He nodded to Javier, who seemed surprised by the Marine's findings. "I will heed your warning, Babe."

Looking from side to side, scoping the entire area, Babe was on high alert. "Someone wired the first and second cars to blow, triggered by the man in the third car with the phone. Threat eliminated. You need to find three more black Suburbans, just like those, and then give me the address of the hangar. The courtesy van can take you to a Chevy dealer or rental car so you can get the new vehicles. I'm not sure I can remove the bombs quickly and time is of the essence. Use the courtesy van driver and two hotel personnel to drive the other vehicles. Have your drivers act like security; I'm thinking they are up for the job anyway, as a best guess. I'll meet you at the hangar."

As suggested, Javier and his men went to the Chevy dealer, and Babe continued in the courtesy van to the hangar. He drove through the gate and to a hangar one over from the meeting place. Just with his naked eye, Babe saw two men standing outside the door, three on the roof, sniper ready. He sidled up to the far side of the building and could hear irritated bellowing voices in Spanish coming from within. He adjusted his phone to the mirror app. Holding his phone to the side of the window, he saw a short, round man checking his watch every few seconds. From what little Spanish he knew, he figured the ranting was because the phone call they were waiting for was late. Babe figured it was Donatello who became more agitated by the second. From his limited sightline, there were six men plus the round squatty barker, three on the roof and two out front.

Babe lightly trilled his fingers on the metal wall just around the corner from the two men guarding the door. One approached while the other stood attentive. *Perfect.* Guard one rounded the corner into the big man. Babe torsioned his neck in a blink, laid him quietly, and relieved him of his AK-47, ankle Sig Sauer, and another pistol in an underarm holster. The man was about six feet tall. Babe hoped his partner had not been that discerning, and he backed around the corner, glancing upward. He knew that would reflexively get the other guard to start looking up. He heard the steps approaching, "Juan, what you looking at, man? I don't see nothing besides they got it covered up there." The man was close enough. Babe felt he could take him out with a quick jut of the gun to the head, at least long enough to give him an edge and time to eliminate the threat. "Hey, Juan—" Babe turned quickly, jabbing the gun's stock into the man's temple. In one fluid movement, he eliminated the problem. The three on the roof were presenting a problem. He knew how to scale up, but the racket would have caused a stir; besides, he had on ridiculous shoes with no grip and a fucking suit, not the most efficient attire to advance an attack. He didn't have any equipment, and while he was confident he could find a vantage point to pick them off from another roof, he couldn't maintain stealth or the element of surprise, starting an all-out blaze ten to one, not great odds.

He called Javier. "Boss, you got a cluster fuck over here. Three motherfuckers on the roof, I can't get to them dressed like this, and there were two guards by the door, but I eliminated that issue. Your boy has six men inside with him. I suggest you forego your meeting and either head back to the hotel or hop on your jet. I haven't secured it yet. Which one is yours?"

Javier seemed calm, not an intonation of disgust or aggravation. "Return to the hotel."

Fuck, more time away from Trinity. What if she had given up on him? He wouldn't blame her. His feisty little woman had needs; how she accomplished quenching her sexual appetite before they began their tryst was something he didn't want to contemplate, but now the thought of her with another man fueled anger from deep inside. Would she wait for him? Those kinds of ideas didn't offer anything good; they only filled him with even more desire to get back to her and incited boundless frustration. He may take Javier up on the offer of a call girl. He needed to nix the frustration he had building inside. He made his way to the courtesy van and headed back to the hotel.

Michael jumped right in the minute Tony, the chef from the restaurant, walked away and told Rainie about the call with William, a.k.a. Mateo. "You have to tell Trinity, Michael. Bethany told me she stays in her room. She's dropped weight, and Mrs. Noelle has her going to Mass every day, saying the Rosary all day, every day—the poor girl. I'm gonna leave a note at Louie's for her to call me. I don't want to stop by the house; I don't know her family well enough, but if I leave a note, maybe they'll call her, and she'll pick it up. Two birds with one stone—get her out of the house and learn that he's alive." Reluctantly, Michael agreed.

Trinity and Gunner pulled up to the construction site. Glenn was coming out of the trailer, and Gunn took off running toward him. He welcomed the pooch's affection. "Hey, where y'at?" He called out to Trinity. He walked over and gave her a hug. "I was worried when Babe didn't show up for work after his week off, but Bethany tells me that Babe has gone missing. Is that true?" Trinity nodded as the tears began to well in her eyes. He held her. "If anybody can take care of himself, you know it's your man. He's never shown an angry side here, but I imagine it's freakin' scary when it appears, and I pity the poor son-of-a-bitch on the other side of his fist. Grab a seat in the AC. I'll be but a minute, hon." Trinity went into the trailer. Her imagination toyed with her. She could smell Babe. It's what he carried home, a scent captured in his clothes— concrete, iron, dirt, dust, and sweat. She missed him and felt a void in her soul.

A few minutes later, Glenn returned. Trinity was looking at the blueprints on his desk. "When y'all gonna finish this? I bet it's taking a toll not having Vic here. I know it's taking a toll here." She put her hand over her heart. "It feels so long, Glenn. What if he's dead?"

Glenn stopped the train of thought, saying he wasn't; he felt sure. She mentioned that the cartel had him, and she could see his face take on a pale. *That's right, Glenn, he might be dead,* the thought zoomed through her mind. He was curious why she would think that. She told him the story about the Marine helo pilot that came to see him. She babbled for an hour, painting the picture of the desperate situation. Glenn was the first to take her seriously and repeatedly apologized for discounting her apprehension. "Mama's got me saying the Rosary all day, every day. I don't know what good that's doing. I thought coming here might help my mood, and I think by you listening and taking me seriously, I might feel better, not good, but purged of the doom and gloom trapped inside of me, if that makes sense." Glenn said he and Bethany would pray for him and for her to find peace. "I think I might swing by Louie's."

Louie's felt more filling than anywhere else without Babe. She could picture him sitting at the end of the bar and, in his deep voice, '*Two fingers Glenlivet, ma'am.*' She flirtatiously rattled back, '*My two fingers or yours,*' it brought a melancholy smile to her face. Her heart filled with butterflies. *Would she ever see him again?* Those feelings sunk into her gut, leaving a heavy imprint, making her want to vomit. Trinity had to fight with everything she had not to break into tears. Undoubtedly, everyone would have heard the Hulk, as they called him, had split. Did they know he'd been abducted and was probably, by this time, dead?

Samantha, the bosomy blonde, hurried from behind the bar. "*Girrl,* it is good to see you. We've missed you something fierce. Sorry to hear your man left you; bastards, they're all turds on legs. Don't choo worry; we'll get you back in the saddle in no time." Some of her regular old-timers were hanging at the bar, and it was only a couple of hours past midday. Somebody should have watered their drinks or occupied them with clever conversation. *Unethical Samantha* was all she could think. They would've been far more sober on her watch and perhaps ordering lunch. "Finn's been working your shifts, and we got a new permanent busser plus a couple of part-time cocktail runners. Shep has stepped up the service, he says, no one could hustle the bar like you." She knew he'd said it in a complimentary manner, but she never thought of herself as hustling the bar, more like taking care of her clientele.

Shep came from the back of the house. "Co'mere, my girl. You, dawlin', are a sight for sore eyes. Da rest of the crew don't understand we need to keep our old guys under control. We've had day after day drunks and been more fights over Sam's titties. She don't know I know, but I do; she's been earning side money in the pisser." Trinity had heard rumors in the past but had not seen the decadent whoring for herself, thus chalking it up to ugly gossip. She would have called the girl out from the get-go. Louie's wasn't a whorehouse; it was an institution of the city filled with history and class.

"Can I get my job back? I won't fall to pieces and make a scene. I promise to get business back in the groove." Her heart seemed to lighten a smidge. The heat in her chest from being there dulled the pain, and her racing, trepidatious heartbeat slowed to a light sashay. "I'll share my shifts with Finn. I don't wanna cut him out if that's okay."

Shep ran his hand under his chin, pulling his jowls into a face cleavage. He thought for a moment, then nodded. "Y'all gonna have to work it for bigger tips. Pull him into your bottle-spinning baton-twirling schtick, ya know, like dat movie. Neva mind, way before your time, dawlin'. Oh, by the way, I got a note for ya." He went to the back office; she followed close behind. He handed her the envelope; she buzzed past him and sat in his chair.

"Don't mind?" she asked, raising her eyebrows. For the first time in weeks, she felt perky. Trinity examined the envelope; it was from an interior decorating firm in Metairie. The penmanship wasn't familiar. She was nervous but opened it sliding her finger through the fold.

Trinity,

I know your world is upside down right now. Babe is alive, and that's a fact. I can't explain; besides, it's too long of an explanation. My source is impeccable and is doing what he can to get your guy home. A big shot in a cartel, I don't know what their title is, but he has kept your Marine as a sort of bodyguard. The frustrating thing is that no one knows for how long. Keep the faith; you'll get him back. Live your life with the knowledge that one day he'll be back. Take care.

Rainie

Trinity read the message a few times. She called Dr. Landry's office. "Hi. This is Trinity Noelle. By any chance, do you have Rainie's cell? I lost my phone and all my contacts." She lied. "I am trying to reach her about a job she's doing for us." The woman on the other side of the phone was hesitant and put her on hold.

Minutes later, Dr. Landry picked up the call. "Are you okay, Trinity?" She said yes and said she needed to speak with Rainie. Going through Mike's mind was, how did Rainie get a message to Trinity so fast? Leave it to his wife to stoke a fire. He called out the number. "Trinity, if my wife s proposes some ludicrous plan, stay clear. She's a fabulous woman but sometimes gets into tight spots, and you don't want to go down the rabbit hole with her. Trust me. Take care, Trinity." The call ended. All she could figure was she didn't sound convincing enough to the receptionist, and now Dr. Landry knew Rainie had contacted her. Fingers crossed, it wouldn't stir up a hornet's nest between them.

She entered the numbers, and it went to a voice message. Trinity explained who she was, that she had received the letter, and asked if they could talk.

NOT MY PARADISE

*T*wo more days passed, and Babe was done with the solitude and waiting. He heard someone knock on Noir's door. He could detect a man's voice and an occasional laugh. *Friends?* They spoke in French. Babe had seen all the movies the hotel had to offer, even the risqué ones, which made him want Trinity even more. He didn't need to watch sex; he had a pictorial rolling in his mind of Trinity, her body, her smile, her laugh, and her insane sexual prowess. Would it be cheating if Babe paid for sex; he debated the thought in his mind. But then, reverse it, if she had paid for a service, quickly erasing the idea; she wasn't one to hire for pleasure, where he often had, which was his M.O. until Trinity. He was even bored with jacking; *what a pathetic state of affairs.* There had been lean times before, but he was at war, and his mind was preoccupied with staying alive or taking out the enemy.

Babe was just about to ask Noir to arrange entertainment when there was a knock on the door between the rooms. He was shocked by the person on the other side. Somewhere in the recesses of his mind, Babe felt like he'd seen the man before, but where, when, no, it was unlikely. Noir introduced him as William LaSalle, someone he knew from years back. They had run into each other in the lobby. *Lobby? And I can't leave my room without Noir, no, I can. I said I wouldn't, two different things entirely. I'd been long gone if it weren't for Trinity's safety.* The whole situation began pissing him off more and more. Noir had a string of entertainment, almost a different woman every night, but that was his business.

"I am to understand you are Captain Vicarelli? Please call me William. How has your stay been at this magnificent resort?" Babe wasn't up for an idle chat. What did this man want? He seemed to be nice enough, but something was off about him. He was wiser than your basic civilian; he had that twinkling of knowing things in his eyes. Nothing escaped him. After their brief conversation, William concluded by saying Trinity, while longing for him, was otherwise well. The hackles went up. The man was maybe six feet tall and had a long braid of graying blond hair with weirdly light eyes. He looked like one of those peace and love characters portrayed in some of the recent movies he'd watched—although nothing stoned about him.

"Sir, what do you know of Trinity? You certainly don't look like someone she'd kick around with, and I truly cannot see you hanging out with Antoine Noelle. No offense."

The older man had a gleeful smile. "I've been to Louie's a time or two and just wanted to tell you, that's all, nothing more. She'll be waiting for you when you return to New Orleans, but until then, I suggest you enjoy the paradise before you. Pleasures abound. Who knows how long you'll be a guest, a week, a month, a year?" He spread his arms in a fluid wave, like making a presentation.

Babe's face took on a cold, lifeless expression. "Sir, not my idea of paradise, and if all your message served was information, thanks for the words. I suspect there is far more to you, sir, than meets the eye." A glimmer appeared in William, like a naughty little boy; it was evident that he wasn't just some friend. No, he was a messenger to let Babe know Trinity was well. He wondered if she had received a head's up and that there wasn't a definitive time frame. *A year?* The entire interaction spoke volumes about Noir. He wasn't necessarily what he appeared to be, maybe he posed as Javier's trustworthy homeboy, but someone else held his strings, and Babe suspected it was William La Salle.

Trinity waited for Rainie to call her back, figuring once she listened to the message and discovered from whence the call came, she'd jump right on it. She stared at the phone as if willing it to ring, but silence. Five minutes passed, then ten, onto fifteen. She was getting the sense that the call would never come.

A rumble and clatter of feet came from the door between the kitchen and the bar. Finn came bolting through the door. She jumped up, thinking something was amiss. He ran over to her, wrapping his arms around her. "I can't believe it," he said amidst gaspy breaths. "Oh, my God, it is so good to see you. Girl, you've had me freaked the fuck out. S'cuse the f-bomb, but you have." He kissed her big on the cheek. "I've missed you. How's the big guy? People gossiped and acted like he bolted, but I know better; he's in love with you and has been eva since he saw you." He kissed her on the other cheek. She was startled by his exuberance.

Trinity explained her conversation with Shep and the need to generate more income if they both tended bar. She mentioned the show and that they'd have to give it a go to both have a job. They needed to put on a show, not just tend bar. The better the performance, the greater the tips. Finn could hardly contain his excitement. "Finn, you know where I live? I was hoping you could come over and watch a movie with me. It's called *Cocktail*. Shep doesn't think I know the movie, but he forgets I'm the youngest of seven. Neville's in his forties and had the hots for whoever the chick was in the movie, so I've seen it bunches. I know you gotta get to work, and I'm heading out. What time are you out of school tomorrow?" He mentioned that he had finished his semester and was somewhat available. They agreed to meet at her place at one the next day.

Rainie's phone rang, and it was Trinity again. "Rainie Landry." She abruptly answered.

"This is Trinity, but I guess you know since I've been blowin' up your phone. I got the note. Can we get together tomorrow or the next day? I'm going back to work; I have to; I'm losing my mind. I just want a few minutes of your time, Mrs.—"

"Only if you call me Rainie, and yes, where do you want to meet?" Rainie looked at Michael with an arched eyebrow. Rainie gave her directions to their home, and they decided to meet the following day at ten. That gave Trinity enough time to talk and return home for the movie with Finn.

Babe waited until he heard the door close behind William LaSalle. "Noir?"

Besides the Marine tats, the two men were nearly identical in their bodies. Noir was nowhere near as weather-worn in the face as Babe, but both were equally intimidating with severe dark hair, closely groomed beards, and rarely a smile to grace their faces. Noir wore a wife beater and lounge pants, whereas Babe dressed in a tee shirt, jeans, and running shoes. "You need something?"

"A fucking year? Did I hear that right?" Babe had a slight scowl pulling his mouth downwards on one side with his fists tightly balled as he paced. "I have a lady friend, and if I'm gone a year, she's not gonna wait around for my sorry ass." He shoved his hands in his pockets. "What the fuck?" He whipped his face toward Noir.

With a voice of velvet, the other piece to the bookends replied. "It will all come to an end. My being here has been a favor for a dear friend. I have a wife, a son, and a daughter. I get the impatience; this isn't even my rodeo, chief. I'm here to ensure your protection." He started to turn back toward his room.

Babe was trying to wrap his mind around the whole thing. *For my protection, what?* "Wait, who gave you the orders?" Noir shrugged, and it was apparent he had no plan to reveal that information. "You're married, yet you've been hosing a different woman every night?" Babe shook his head. "Not judging, you do you."

Noir shrugged a shoulder and continued walking toward his room. "It passes the time; besides, I don't need calluses on my hand," he laughed and closed the door. He opened it quickly, "You want company tonight? Just share a dinner; you don't need to share anything else. They come fully equipped, in case you're wondering."

Babe passed on the idea for the night. Repeatedly he said, "A year, shit." Then, he wondered what Trinity would be doing for a year. What did she do before they were an item? Friends with twists? Thinking about that wrenched his gut, spewing acid up his throat. He knocked on the closed door. She hadn't had a boyfriend that he was aware of, and then the question popped up as before, he didn't know much about her past. *That's right; we were going to talk about all that shit, and then the snake and this nightmare began, so be it.*

"Change of heart?" Noir asked, but Babe shook his head.

"What does your wife do when you're gone that long?" Noir turned his hands up.

"Marine, I don't think about it. Why think about what you can't control? My wife loves me, I know that, and she also knew what she was getting into that my job might require me to be gone for long periods of time. The first few times are hard, but you get over it—anything to pass the time. I eat, read, exercise, run, and have frequent visitors. Personally not into television or movies. We should be hearing something in the next day."

"And the check's in the mail." Babe retorted sarcastically. "Order me whatever you're having for dinner, and I'll take it from there, so make sure she's good with either."

Noir turned at his door. "Blonde, brunette, any preference?"

"Just not Creole; mine is perfect." Noir raised his chin doing the guy-thing acknowledgment.

Babe returned to rigorous exercise, down on the floor, up to his feet, back down, as though it were a race against time. He looked through the drawers to see if there was any reading material. He'd read and re-read the magazines filled with Miami's entertainment and adventure offerings, not that he would have an opportunity to explore, nor did he want to. The only notion was getting home and back to Trinty.

The last drawer he opened had a never cracked Bible. The binding was stiff, and it creaked as he opened it. The pages were thin to the point it was hard to separate one from another. He pushed the pillows back against the headboard. Somewhere in his mind, he remembered one of the priests from school commenting that people find drudgery in reading the Bible because they start at the beginning; it was best to start with Psalms, Songs of Someone or Something, or the Gospels.

Psalms it was. He flipped through, dampening each corner, pulling apart stuck page from page. Finally, he turned to Psalms. "Blessed is the one who does not walk in the step with the wicked."(Psalms1:1 NIV) *So much for that*, which once again begged the question, was he a good or bad man? Reading the verse and applying it to his situation, he was most definitely and unequivocally walking in step with the wicked. Maybe somewhere, it might qualify the instruction by adding a word about protecting a person from their nemesis. He continued reading, "or stand in the way that sinners take or sit in the company of mockers, but whose delight is in the law of the Lord, and who meditates on his law day and night."(Psalms 1:1-2 NIV) God was giving him an out, a way to correct his path, but he wasn't sure if he could change his leopard spots just yet. He was still in a job that required breaking a Commandment or two. Babe remembered some of them. Dazing off, he began reciting what he could visualize on the wall above the chalkboard at his high school. Holding up his hands, he managed eight and was positive he had them out of order. He resumed reading, absorbing and contemplating the words and enjoying the content; Trinity would be proud and surprised. *Yep, I'm one of the big sinners, no doubt. Nope not ready to repent.* The book was like a manual but with people doing life things, not sheer mechanics and maneuvering. Babe read until there was a knock on the door. *Crap, I forgot to cancel.* "Hang on," he called aloud. He was still fully clothed and went to the door.

Room service rolled the cart in, followed by a buxom blonde with the same look as Samantha—attractive in a cheap way—*tips for tits, kinda girl.*

"Heyyy, handsome." She spoke, trying for a sultry intonation. *Mission failed.* Trinity was the real deal; this girl was looking to earn a few bucks, and he felt more in the mood to keep reading. Faking a smile, he pulled a chair out from the small table in the room. She batted her eyes and sat. "Divine and scrumptious—and the food too," forcing a more than fake giggle. *Gimme a break.* She arched one eyebrow and ran her tongue across her teeth. "Lance, I'm Jacquelyn, but my friends call me Jackie." *Lance, what the fuck, fucking Lance? That was a name for some suave sophisticate. Why not George or Steve or Mike, fucking Lance. I owe Noir one.*

"We better eat, Jackie, before our dinner gets cold. I'm not a big talker." He half grinned.

"Baby, you don't have to say a word; just let me know what you want from me. How can I relax you?" She lowered her eyes for an attempt at coy. *Failed miserably.* "Just tell this girl how I can make your night." *Leave* was all he could think. He started eating, looking up at her between bites. "I heard about your friend, Antonio," she twitched her head to Noir's room. "He wore my friend out." She giggled. "I don't wear out that easy." She winked at him. *Let this night be over.* Jackie took a few bites, then walked around the room, looking out the window. "Nice view." She spied the Bible on his bed and stopped dead in her tracks. "Don't tell me you're one of those. I don't need no soul-saving, honey. Now tell me exactly what you want, and we can skip the small talk."

The answer came so clearly to him. "I thought you could read to me. No?" He chuckled inside, knowing the answer already.

"Mister, is it a fuck or suck, or do you want me to watch you get off. If it's none of the above, then I'm outta here. We ain't reading the Bible for damn sure." He shrugged a shoulder. "I'm paid in full for two hours. Lemme fuck some of that Holy Roller out of you." He had so much pent-up angst that his body could use the release, but maybe if he played by the rules, the Supposed God would get him home sooner than later. He cocked a smile and shook his head at her. "Whateva!" She huffed out of the room, pissed.

Babe laid back down and continued reading. At the beginning of Psalms were two paragraphs highlighting the assumed author and speculated timeframe. He could identify with some of the things that David felt. David was a passionate man that didn't always have life going his way. Babe could relate. After finishing all of Psalms, he got in the shower around midnight. His thoughts were of nothing but Trinity. Since he hadn't given in to the temptation of the call girl, he took advantage of the shower, thinking of his lady.

Babe's sleep was deep, filled with good dreams and happy places with Trinity; the nightmares of his missions gone wrong and childhood abuse had vanished for the time being, maybe because he was living a bad dream. It was his new reality.

He woke around six and started what he could of his morning ritual. Noir knocked. "Marine, you up?" Babe looked to the side as he crunched upward. "I told you today might be the day. Dress and meet me in my room in one hour. Oh, she any good?"

"Not really, just your basic rosy palm. Lance? What the fuck? I look like a Lance to you, An-to-ni-o?" Noir laughed.

Rainie's house was beautiful, like a real family kind of home, with a feel similar to the home her parents raised the seven of them. The gorgeous redhead met Trinity at her car and walked her to the backyard, through the gate, past the pool, and into the office. "Nice setup, ya got. Beautiful home. You and Dr. Landry have five children? I'm the caboose of seven." All she wanted to ask was Babe's whereabouts and how did she know he was okay?

Rainie commented that the house was perfect for them, and yes, they had four boys and a daughter. She opened the door, "Something to drink? I know all you want to hear is how I know Babe is okay. I can't tell you all the ins and outs, but here is what I can say." Rainie sat behind the desk, indicating Trinity to sit on one of the two chairs facing her.

"Michael and I have a friend closely connected to a cartel; I should say, years back, he was involved. And while he has—" she stopped. Trinity could see the gears shifting, Rainie wondering what she could and could not say. "He is in a different line of work, or retired, might be better. He still has a few underground contacts and has planted one in the organization that has Babe. Some big pow-wow is coming up, like jostling for position and control, and one of the guys is worse than the other. Although, truthfully, they are all fucking crazy and evil." She sipped off the glass on the desk. "Anyway, our friend has put his person in the game to purposefully keep your man safe. The unknown here is how long they will want him. Judging from Babe's and my conversation at Bethany's, he's one fierce guy, like Special Ops Terminator shit, and they're not going to want to let him go. The one ace in the hole is that my friend's contact wants nothing to do with the business. He's on loan, for lack of a better description, because of his skills and intelligence for this particular meeting. I think they suspect similar attributes appealing with your guy, plus his kickass training. Jeez, Louise." Rainie rolled her eyes.

Trinity held onto her every word. "So how long is long?"

The red-haired beauty shrugged her shoulders and turned her hands up. "Sorry, I have no idea. Babe will be home as soon as he can; I know that. He loves you, Trinity. Look, do what ya gotta do while you wait, but don't give up on him. He will make it back to you."

Trinity's eyes glossed with unfallen tears. "The uncertainty is gonna kill me, but thanks for the info, and bartenders are great at keeping things confidential, even over one pour." She gave a half-hearted smile, bid farewell, and headed back to her place in the hotel.

Trinity made it home with enough time to look up the movie and fast-forward to a part where Tom Cruise and Bryan Brown performed behind the bar. She picked up a mostly empty bottle, tossed it in the air, and caught it behind her back. Trinity grabbed an unopened bottle and tried again with success, but barely, so went for it again and again until it was perfect. She felt confident that she could teach Finn.

With the television queued, she was ready and started cleaning her room, talking aloud and reciting the conversation. "Warning, Babe, my room is a mess," she changed her voice to a huskier manly impersonation, "You're a fucking slob." She picked up the pillow and took a deep breath; she could still smell his scent making her heart shatter into pieces. "No, I'm not crying anymore." Before leaving her parent's house, she had put the Rosary over her head, wearing it beneath her top. She pulled it out, kissed it, and said a little prayer until her phone rang. "Thanks, yes, send him back." Trinity opened the door and waited for Finn to show.

It looked like his head was on a swivel as he made the corner. "This place is cool. Man, I didn't know this even existed, but wow." She hugged him.

"Come on in, sport. Let's get to the lessons and rehearsal."

He looked around at her apartment. "This is the deal, damn, girl."

Finn took a bottle of Sprite out of his back pocket and sat on the sofa, ready to learn. They sat and watched the television as the actors did their schtick behind the bar. She cocked her head and smiled at him. "Whatcha think?"

He turned his head toward her. "I'm totally down for it. Shit, we can even do better. How bout you even get into some Coyote Ugly on the bar? I can lift you easy enough." His eyes twinkled, "Totally down." Finn saw the bottle sitting on the side table and started mimicking the actions on the screen. He nearly missed, laughed, and said, "Maybe we need plastic bottles to start. Nah, just kiddin', I got this. What we need is some music."

Trinity tapped her phone; the music came through inset speakers. They practiced the routine for a couple of hours, then sat exhausted. "Trinity, I say we start tonight in front of our bar flies. Start early, and then we'll be in stride when the house fills. Your thoughts?" He guzzled the Sprite, watching her. The corners of his eyes crinkled with excitement, like getting ready to meet a blind date with thrilling apprehension.

Her head bounced with a nodding yes. "Sure, why not. Don't get all razzle-dazzle and drop the bottle, especially the expensive whiskey, vodka, and gin. You hear, don't be too cocky." He did a few dance moves right out of the eighties, doubling her in hilarity. He fell back on the couch, coughing with laughter and gasping for air. It had been a while since she'd laughed like that, and it felt good. It didn't mean she wasn't missing Babe, but she felt alive like she joined the land of the living.

Babe dressed but not in the business attire he'd worn before. The point—if they needed his skills, the suit would have immobilized him; it was such a confining ensemble. He donned a black Henley top and joggers with his running shoes.

Once ready, he knocked and entered Noir's room. Javier, three of his men, and Noir sat around conversing, probably about the meeting, and glancing at the news. Javier spoke, "Had a good night, I hear. You ready for today? Informal, I see." He pointed with a sweeping downward motion at Babe's outfit.

"Practical, sir, and I'm more than ready; that's a promise. Ready to get home." The bossman shrugged with a slight nod. He was non-commital, which Babe took as a disappointing sign.

They continued their discussion; from what Babe could decipher, the sit-down would be in one of the smaller resort meeting spaces. He asked Javier if he wanted him to sweep the premises. The boss said one of his men had already managed, and Javier posted him outside to avoid surprises like hidden weapons or assassins. Babe would have felt better walking the room prior to the meeting, but Javier felt comfortable with the security. Like in any situation, there were always those people that one could pay off for the right price. It amazed him the lack of integrity that enveloped the world; he understood Javier seeking him and Noir, both being independent without attachment in the cartel world. Then again, where were Noir's loyalties, and who the fuck was the stoner-looking guy? Babe instinctually knew the man was not what he seemed.

Javier stood, straightened his jacket, and proceeded toward the door. Two of his men went before him and one behind, with Noir flanking the left and Babe on the right. It was like the fucking secret service. Everyone was in business attire, and he knew he stuck out like a sore thumb, but that's how he rolled. Hopefully, the casual form-fitting clothing would result in a light frisk keeping the knife in his sock undetected.

When they got to the door, Noir stepped to the side, and the guy holding post took his place. The elevator down the hall glided open almost silently. The entourage with Mr. Vargas was identical to Javier's. One of the Vargas guys stepped to the side. Before entering the room, Noir frisked each of the adversary's people, and the Vargas man checked Javier's guys. As hoped, the man looked at Babe with a smirk and waved him through with a light pass over him, almost an insult. Everyone took their seat. The table lacked space for one chair, so the casual misfit sat away from the table. From his angle, Babe could see almost all faces. He watched and calculated what moves he could make if a situation presented itself. A wall made of glass created a picturesque view overlooking the beach and water. Babe found it odd that cartel superstars would leave themselves so vulnerable, but the meeting went as planned, with fake jovial banter to begin.

Donatello opened the serious talk, "I heard your Pensacola operation got closed down. True?" Javier nodded once slowly, briefly closing his eyes. "So, you're looking for a piece of my Miami business? If I were to be so inclined to allow this, there would be a defined area, not one block off any side, and twenty-five percent off the top for my generosity and good faith with your organization. You forget, Javier, I had this territory long before Mateo was Alejandro's boy, so you got some balls coming here cap in hand. Out of respect for Mateo, God rest his soul; they all made the Sign of the Cross; I will agree to those conditions."

Javier sat quietly with his hands steepled in front of him, elbows on the table. He touched his fingers to his lips, then looked up. "Fifteen percent, and that's generous, I was thinking more like ten, but since you have shown such diplomacy, I will go the extra five, depending on the territory you relinquish." Donatello looked down and slowly shook his head.

"No. It is, as I said, twenty-five."

"Eighteen percent, including the Bahamas." Javier stretched his chin upward.

"Why do you insult me like that? It'll be an all-out war and much blood in the streets. I will come down to twenty, and no Bahamas—out of the question. The blood in the streets will be on your hands."

The ice in the room was palpable even though sweat trickled down a couple of the men's faces. There was an edge, a hard, dangerous edge. Babe detected one of Vargas' men bring his foot across his knee as though relaxing. Too close if there were an undetected knife or holster. Not that he was second-guessing Noir, but if he moved again, the man would have a knife protruding from his arm, perhaps nicking the artery. If not, it would at least cause a bit of pandemonium. Enough to distract with time to torque one, maybe two; then hell would open up. Hopefully, it was just an itch on the guy's leg. In his peripheral vision, he could see Noir watching him. No way was he going to avert his eyes. Tensions were mounting.

Javier ran his hands down his face, holding them in place for a second, then accidentally knocked his pen, provided by the hotel, with his elbow onto the floor. As he bent to pick it up, the sound of shattering glass penetrated the air, and the repetitious studdering of automatic guns deafened the yelling. Men dove helter skelter. Vargas sat still in his chair with his head on his chest and a blooming wet patch growing on his black shirt. The spray of bullets tore holes in his jacket. Babe didn't skip a beat;

he saw Noir protectively on top of Javier and did what he does best to the two closest Vargus men, shattering their necks inside five seconds, if that. He threw one of the remaining men, who sat frozen with his mouth agape, on the ground with his foot on his neck and had the other in a headlock. The shooters hit one of Javier's men, his right arm riddled with gunshots. They knew it would be moments before the alarms sounded, the police dispatched, and the once tranquil scene looked like a scene from a Scorsese movie.

Javier's entourage ran, ducking into one of the black Suburbans. A driver was sitting with the engine running, and they took off. All their possessions remained in the guest rooms. The driver sped to the airport, and within minutes of getting to the hangar, they were on the jet taxiing out and taking off. "Babe, your Commander Deary was right. You are one fierce fucker." Once at cruising altitude, they fixed drinks. Babe poured a three-finger glass of whiskey, grabbed a napkin, and held it on his side. Quickly, Babe's blood soaked through; he'd taken a hit just above his right hip, hopefully not hitting any vital organs.

"Hey, Chief," Babe asked Javier, "Where we headed?" He lightly touched his lips to the tumbler with his free hand.

"Cartagena."

Babe, disheartened, gulped the rest of the drink and poured a second.

A GIRL'S GOTTA DO

*T*rinity and Finn walked down to Louie's, both excited about the new arrangement. The music from the pub reverberated out the open bank of doors. He took her hand, "Okay, you and me, we got this." He spun, skipping backward. "Everybody in the Quarter's gonna hear about our amazing show, and we'll have guests lining outside the door. I'm telling you, Trinity, if you get up on the bar and dance, our tips will be phe-nom. Girl, with that tight little body of yours—"

She stopped him abruptly. "Finn, get a grip and don't go talkin' about my tight little body. You know me better than that. Besides, you make me feel like those leches that come in the bar sometimes. Eww! You know how old I am?"

He chuckled, "Yeah, you made twenty-eight on your last birthday. I'm twenty-two, gonna be twenty-three, so you're not like that much older than me, 'sides, I meant no offense. I know you're Babe's girl." She sucked in a deep breath. "I'm not hitting on you. No way." He grinned. "We're like dance partners, ya know? Kinda Dancing with the Stars." They both found his analogy humorous.

Trinity tottered her head back and forth from shoulder to shoulder. "Okay, yeah. Sorry. I'm in a bad headspace right now, and this has been the most fun I've had since the abduct—" She stopped short.

"Abduction? What like the Hulk? Who in their right mind would want to fuck with him?" His skips slumped into more of a shuffle as he ran his hand through his hair. Trinity thought he was about to cry; that was all she

179

needed. He became silent as he slowed the pace to Louie's.

She sucked in another deep breath and told him that the performance had to happen and that they didn't practice for nothing. She would've never invited his scrawny ass to her place if she didn't think it would be a good move for Louie's. "So, shake it off. I have to."

Once inside Louie's, the regulars clapped when they saw her. The cat calls rang throughout the place. One of the regular barflies, missing most of his teeth and probably nearing seventy-five, spoke with tears in his eyes. "Baby, I've missed your beautiful smile and a good Old Fashion; that blonde-haired girl can't make an Old Fashion to save her life."

Finn clocked in, and Trinity went behind the bar relieving the early-hour barkeep. She cranked the music up so it was louder. Finn joined her behind the bar. First order up: Trinity grabbed the Vodka and flipped it in the air while swaying to the music. It didn't take long for the bellies at the bar to catch on, and the whole place started to rock, drawing attention from the street and more customers. The tips increased the more their antics became sassier.

Shep came from the back to see what the big fuss was in the front of the house. The smile that grew on his face shone like the sun. His cheeks turned a ruby red, and his laugh came straight from his belly. They raked the money in; it would be a good night for Louie's, the bussers, the wait staff, and Team Dynamo. He headed back to the kitchen.

Just after midnight, Trey and Max, two NOPD detectives, entered the bar. Max nudged Trey, and they both watched in amusement. After mixing a flux of orders, Finn stood behind Trinity and lifted her onto the bar. The magic of her dancing brought on cheers, catcalls, clapping, and a contagious enthusiasm that provoked couples to start dancing. It was party time at Louie's Pub. Shep peeked out and saw Trey and Max approaching them with concern. "Detectives, everything okay?"

Trey beamed, "Absolutely. There was a report that y'all had some rowdiness in here, and since we finished at a crime scene down the street, I thought we'd check out the call. This place is hoppin'. I don't think I've ever seen it this wild." Trey looked at the end of the bar. His eyebrows drew in close, wrinkling his forehead. "Still no word from our Marine?" Shep crossed his arms over his round stomach, stuck his bottom lip out, and shook his head sadly. "Wow. The whole thing is so strange. What's Trinity say about it?" Trey stood with his hands on his hips.

Almost off in a daze watching the customers, "We don't talk about it. She's been out weeks, maybe months; nonetheless, a long time. Tonight's her first night back. The word is, he's dead, so I don't push her. Y'all were there the night the big guy was taken, right? Y'all ain't heard nothin'?"

Trey looked glum. "Sadly, no, other than it had something to do with a cartel hit."

"Yeah, that's what the word is on the block. It's a damn shame. The man fights in wars and then comes home, and what happens? Sickening, but the naysayers are saying he just skipped town. I call bullshit on that, not the way he loves my niece. Gotta get to the back, boys. Thanks for stopping in." Trey left for home, and Max left for God knows where, probably a frozen dinner, a beer, and falling asleep in his recliner in front of the television.

As the clock drew close to three thirty, most of the crowd had petered out, and the chaos left with the last group of rowdy men and women. She found it amusing that several women hit hard on Finn. He was adorable, like Ralph Macchio in The Karate Kid, only an Irish Channel version. "Hey, boo, you ready to call it a night?" she asked. She finished counting the tips, and the tally came to over seven hundred dollars. "Finn, I don't know if we can keep this up night after night. I'm exhausted." He grabbed his top shirt and clocked out.

"Girl, I'm gonna walk you home all the way. Who knows what piece of shit is hanging around to swipe you. You were outstanding tonight."

He took her hand as they walked and twirled her under his arm. Their body heat was insane. She looked up at him for a second and touched her lips to his. "Yeah, walk me all the way home. Maybe come in for a bit?"

His heart fluttered momentarily, but he stopped her, looked her dead in the eyes, "You don't gotta do this. It was just a kiss, Trinity. I know where your heart lies. I know who your man is."

"I know, but I need this right now." She said. "You good with that? We'll still be friends tomorrow, even if it never happens again?"

"You bet." Finn agreed.

LIVE, LOVE, OR DIE

*7*he jet touched down, and by that time, Babe had knocked back a few three-finger pours, which dulled the pain from the gunshot, but left his heart aching. He'd have been better off working for Antoine Noelle, doing his dirty work, than being stranded in Cartagena, where he didn't speak the language or know the area or the people. At least with the Marines, there were hard lines, and one knew where they stood and what the Corps demanded. The Marines made it crystal clear about things like rules, honor, and expectations of accountability, not a nest of lies, deception, and betrayal—where a man's word meant nothing.

He could hear the Commander's voice. *Civilian life isn't for everyone, Vicarelli.* What was Deary doing, trying to make a point like 'get your ass back in the Corps?' All he wanted was an everyday life; he'd given all he could; there was nothing left to give. He needed every ounce of intestinal fortitude to make it through this nightmare. What of Trinity? He couldn't blame her for giving up on him. If he made it back to her and she accepted him with loving arms, he'd reconsider working for Antoine and let the mob and the cartel duke it out for him; at least he'd be with her.

"As soon as we get on the compound, I'll have my doctor remove that bullet and mend you up. Once again, you're something else, Marine, a fucking machine. I owe Deary. Babe thought, *No, motherfucker, you owe me. I kept my word; now you keep yours.* The sinking feeling crept into his belly, whispering that the plan had changed and wasn't a one-and-done.

Three cars waited on the tarmac as the jet stopped. The cast of characters deplaned, Javier, indicating the vehicle for Babe to slide into. It was just him and the boss. Babe silently questioned the situation. Javier asked, "How are you feeling?" *Pissed* is what came to mind. *Where is Noir?* "I know you want to get back to your friend, but there is much I can offer you here. You would be a perfect replacement for Seb. I understand you have a Law Degree. Oh, the things I can offer you to sweeten the pot. Women come and go, my friend. She is young with a bright future ahead. She deserves more than an on-again-off-again partner or the wife of a Marine. Think of her." Babe could feel the heat rising up the back of his neck. Commander Deary had spoken too freely with this man, leaving him vulnerable to the one thing he'd have difficulty fighting and would never overcome—guilt.

Babe started analyzing Javier's words; maybe the man had sound advice. Trinity would be far better off than with the likes of him. She was way out of his league; he'd always known it. He needed to let her go and live her life. She'd forget him, fall in love, marry, and have a few children. What kind of father could he be? "So you plan on holding me here? I kept my word and was there for you and your men as I said I would. You said—"

Javier's voice became severe, almost harsh. "I am well aware of what I said." He then lightened up. "Don't be hasty in your decision; think it over. In the meantime, make a list of the things you want. I will see to it." The car flew along the road; a wash of lush green and brightly colored flowers presented an excellent backdrop that should have been paradisal but emphasized his painful thoughts and made the disappointment even more brutal. He loved her beyond reason, and if he needed to step back for her to thrive, he loved her enough to do it. "Think about it, and when you convalesce with a clearer mind, then make your decision. If you want to return to your small apartment and low-paying construction job for a mediocre existence to be with the woman, then so be it. You'll always ride her coattails. I must admit, I don't think of you as a kept man." *You sleazy motherfucker, trying to hit all my buttons. Fuck you,* the thought screamed through his head.

"I need a shower and a bed." The car drove past massive twelve-foot concrete walls topped with razor wire. He could see the tops of beautiful palm trees. The fronds were full and perfectly sculpted, like one would see on a cover of a travel brochure. Slowly the car turned down a short drive, secured by a solid iron gate reinforced with four-inch iron binders held by massive rivets. The monstrous fort-like entrance opened slowly. To the left side of the driveway was a guardhouse; the guard had an automatic machine gun hanging loosely over his shoulder with pistols at his hips. Before them was an ornate iron gate that opened faster than the first. Babe figured this must be Javier's compound. If the walls and security were any indications of the rest of the property, he was sure it would be impressive, maybe impenetrable, but more importantly, inescapable for his purposes.

Babe needed to clear his head. Deary obviously gave Javier all his pressure points, and in the most warped sense, like so much he'd heard about the cartel, this was the most conniving mind fuck he'd ever had.

Armed guards stood throughout the property. If there wasn't a security detail with eyes on, cameras were constantly observing and tracking. Babe felt it inevitable that people monitored possible activity twenty-four-seven. To have so much power and yet feel such vulnerability had to be soul-crushing. Javier had no life, and was that what he was offering? No amount of money would be enough to surrender his freedom. He'd fought too hard to yield. He was going home one way or another.

Babe found it amusing that for all the information people had on him, no one knew about the house on Chestnut or that he had substantial money. He wasn't riding on anyone's coattails, and he'd be damned if he'd relinquish his way of life for the indulgence of another man.

Theirs was the only vehicle to return to the compound. Where were all the other men, especially Noir? What happened to Seb? Whether Javier was accustomed to people questioning his words, Babe didn't give a hearty shit. He'd get the bossman alone and get answers, one way or another.

The clock went off at eleven that morning. Trinity rolled over, and a weight of guilt fell on her heart. Finn was a good guy, and most men wouldn't have agreed to snuggle in bed next to a woman without expecting some sexual interaction. Where the kiss had come from, maybe it was the hype of the night, the thrill of not feeling dead inside, whatever, he was right, it was just a kiss. Her words were beyond the pale after implying so much more bedroom interaction. What she needed was to be held, to fall asleep in someone's arms, to be comforted.

He smiled at her. "Penny for your thoughts?"

"Finn, I'm sorry. I know you probably had a different picture of our after-work adventure, but I didn't know how to say I wanted to be held and snuggled. We're still friends?"

He clasped his hands behind his head and glanced at her quickly. "Truthfully, I don't know if I could have; you belong to Babe. Man, you're hot, no doubt, but you're spoken for, and I'm not that dude that nails a friend's girl. I don't think my hoo-hoo woulda worked." He smiled at her again. She burst into a belly laugh.

"Hoo-hoo? You're a good guy. I'm glad nothing happened besides the kiss, of which I feel guilty as all hell, but if something happens and Babe doesn't come back, or I find out," she shook the thought from her head, "I might be locking lips with you again. That was a nice kiss. We were all in our feelings from the high of the night." She lay silent for a few minutes absorbing the oddity of the encounter, and then bolted straight up, "Oh, my God, your mom must be worried sick."

"While you were taking your shower when we got here, I called her to let her know I wasn't coming home. I may have lied a little. I told her you had too much to drink, and since your trauma with that dude, I felt like I needed to stay at your place, on the sofa." She laid next to him, wrapping her arm around his waist. "I don't wanna give you the wrong impression, Trinity, but I miss The Hulk, too. I think everyone does especially knowing how much y'all love each other. It really scared me when you stayed away from work for so long. I almost passed by your parent's place. I know where they live. Obviously, I didn't."

They stayed in bed for the next hour, talking about his life, his dad's death, his latest girlfriend, and his dreams after college. He was Pre-Law, a fact no one at Louie's knew. She always referred to him as a boy, but he was very much a man. He'd financially helped his mom for three years while in school and working at Louie's. He was more responsible than a lot of older men that she knew. Finn told her he'd spoken to Babe about possibly joining the military, and the big guy advised against it.

"Did you know Babe went to Law School, took the Bar, passed, and then joined the Marines?" She smiled with pride, talking about his accomplishments. He was pretty amazing after all he'd gone through.

"No shit," Finn turned on his side and was expressive as he carried on. "He didn't tell me that, but I didn't tell him I wanted to go into law. I don't know what I told him; I was shocked that he told me to stay in school. I know he thinks the country and the world for that matter is fucked up, 'scuse, but he has definite opinions on things."

It was her turn to giggle, "No shit!" mocking him, "You should hear him talk back to the TV, the commentators, and let one of the generals, one in particular, I can't remember his name, but he loses his shit and says someone needs to put a boot up their butt or deploy them for a few months. He definitely has opinions." She got out of bed and offered to buy him lunch, but he declined. The truth was, she was lonely, and somehow Finn made her feel in touch with Babe.

As he stood at the door to leave, they started talking about plans for the night and their new act, both getting energized and excited for the night to come. Their exuberance was contagious, and they fed off each other. "Go, Finn, now, before we find we're still talking and it's time to go to work. Tell your mom how good you did and thank her for understanding about last night." A warm wave rolled through her body. The positivity gave her hope.

Trinity heard her phone buzzing as it vibrated on her bedside chest. She sprinted to answer, hoping it was Babe; alas, "Hi, Mama. I'm at my apartment." She listened for a few minutes, apologized for leaving Gunner at their house, and promised to get him. "I love you, too. See you in a bit." Gunner was like Trinity and Babe's child. She felt like he kept their relationship alive; suddenly, she felt the weight of being irresponsible. Gunner must've been confused about having both Babe and her disappear. The dog had not been himself since Babe's abduction. She fell back on her bed and pleaded, "Babe, come home, wherever you are. Please, God, help him come home."

Sixteen hundred miles away, Babe was doing everything in his power to return to Trinity. He knew it was going to be an arduous task, but in his heart believed he could make it happen.

The Impossible Lie, book three of the **Fit The Crime** series, continues with Babe, Trinity, the cartel, and all the new friends you've made. Cheers! Be on the lookout!

Many Thanks…

To Doug, my fabulous husband, for his patience with my ever-droning half-thoughts. Sometimes I need the opinion of a man and not just my character's ideas. His encouragement keeps me going when I doubt myself. You are the one that puts up with me getting lost in my head, then throwing the lifeline, pulling me from the world of fiction into reality. Thank you, my love, for believing in me.

To Kaye, Kristen, Nick, John, and Riley (better known as #5), your enthusiasm and encouragement as I start and end books are overwhelming. Your excitement triggers me when I fall into the doldrums. Thank you to my daughters and sons-in-law for your support and love and for liking/sharing my posts.

Thank you, my precious grandkids, for telling everyone you know that your Nana is an author. Y'all keep me in my feelings! Did I get that right? Once you reach eighteen, you can read my books, but until then, I hope you enjoy my PG descriptions of the plots and characters and the back of the books.

To Paige Brannon Gunter, my forever editor, as long as you'll have me. Your advice and suggestions for improvement or other angles of consideration are invaluable. You get me, and you get my characters. Your attention to the nuances and appreciation of the human psyche warms my heart and validates me.

To G. Lee, who consistently catches my comma splices and try as you may, I'll never grasp the concept. I think you finally understand my dialect; what can I say? I'm a NOLA girl, sir.

To K.N. Faulk for pointers in character development and consistency. So, I know you say you love Babe, but just how much—should I be worried? You're as crazy about him as I am. He is indeed one bad-ass m'f-er.

To Julie Agan for all the information about things only a Marine might know, or should I say, the mom of a Marine. Your help has been outstanding, and I hope you are with me for the whole ride.

To Cyrus Wraith Walker, where does one begin with the guru of design? You teach me every dang time. Thank you, sir. I know I change my mind willy-nilly, but it's because you inspire me.

To our men and women in the armed forces and their families, thank you for your service and sacrifice.

To you, my readers, thank you for spreading the word and supporting me in my writing endeavors. Remember to share, comment, and tell your friends to register on my website. **corinnearrowood.com**. Thank you, thank you, thank you. *As always, I wish you love.*

In lieu of a proper bibliography—

The abundance of Marine YouTube videos, articles, and interviews is fantastic. After many hours and months of research, I learned much. I have always appreciated and felt gratitude for our military services, but thanks to my Marine, Captain Babe Vicarelli, I have been pushed to learn even more. The information on PTSD is vast and ever-increasing. The research was eye-opening and heart-wrenching. Words of thanks can never be enough. I must thank again, Julie Agan, who offered to be a beta reader. As a mother of a Marine, she has been a plethora of information from a different angle than my other sources.

The Taliban and Islamist information are from research articles and, more honestly, from my Marine, now FBI friend who will remain nameless out of respect for their privacy. You know who you are. Thank you for sharing some of your horrifying moments of service.

The information about drug and sex trafficking is some scary stuff, and I must admit it keeps me awake some nights. My information came from docuseries on television, articles on the internet, and hours spent in the local library.

All Bible references are from the YouVersion app NIV version and the many years of Bible study. The teachers and pastors are too numerous to list, but I often fall back on Carol Richardson, James Mitchell, Josh Elder, John Chetta, and Chris Fryou, to mention a few.

Other Books by the Author
Censored Time Trilogy
A Quarter Past Love (Book I)

Half Past Hate (Book II)

A Strike Past Time (Book III)

Friends Always

A Seat at the Table

PRICE TO PAY

The Presence Between

Fit the Crime Series
The Innocence Lie

Be On the Look Out for...
Leave No Doubt

The Impossible Lie (Book III of the Fit The Crime series)

Visit my website, corinnearrowood.com, and register to win freebies

Reviews are appreciated

About The Author

According to Me

Local girl to the core. There's nowhere on earth like New Orleans! I am still very much in love with my husband of over thirty-five years, handsome hunk, Doug. I'm a Mom, Nana, and great-Nana. (four kids, thirteen grands, three great-grands) Favorite activities include hanging with the hubs, watching grandkids' games and activities, hiking, reading, and traveling. I am addicted to watching The Premier League, particularly Liverpool—The real football—married to a Brit; what can I say? Living my best life writing and playing with my characters and their stories. I'm a Girl Raised In The South (G.R.I.T.) Perhaps the most important thing about me is my faith in God. All of my characters, thus far, have opened a closed heart to an open one filled with Light. Some take longer than others.

According to the Editors

Born and raised in the enchanting city of New Orleans, the author lends a flavor of authenticity to her books and the characters that come to life in stories of love, lust, betrayal, and murder. Her vivid style of storytelling transports the reader to the very streets of New Orleans with its unique sights, smells, and intoxicating culture.

Printed in the USA
CPSIA information can be obtained
at www.ICGtesting.com
JSHW020422200823
46889JS00001B/9

9 798987 364284